THE SEAGULL

THE SEAGULL

A Comedy in Four Acts

ANTON CHEKHOV

Translated from the Russian by
Richard Nelson, Richard Pevear
and Larissa Volokhonsky

THEATRE COMMUNICATIONS GROUP
NEW YORK
2017

The Seagull is published by Theatre Communications Group, Inc.,
520 Eighth Avenue, 24th Floor, New York, NY 10018-4156

The publication of *The Seagull* by Richard Nelson, Richard Pevear and Larissa Volokhonsky, through TCG's Book Program, is made possible in part by the New York State Council on the Arts with the support of Governor Andrew Cuomo and the New York State Legislature.

TCG books are exclusively distributed to the book trade by Consortium Book Sales and Distribution.

Library of Congress Control Numbers:
2017018396 (print) / 2017020218 (ebook)
ISBN 978-1-55936-549-9 (trade paper) / ISBN 978-1-55936-871-1 (ebook)
A catalog record for this book is available from the Library of Congress.

Book design and composition by Lisa Govan
Cover design by John Gall

First Edition, October 2017
Second Printing, February 2023

CONTENTS

INTRODUCTION

The opening night of *The Seagull* on October 17, 1896, at the Alexandrinsky Theatre in St. Petersburg, was a disaster. The audience hissed, jeered, booed; the actors were completely disconcerted and could hardly speak their lines. Chekhov watched the first two acts, but fled backstage at the intermission and left the theater and Petersburg after the performance, swearing he would never write another play. "It was a failure I couldn't have imagined in my worst dreams," he wrote three weeks later to his friend, the liberal lawyer and writer Anatoly Koni. "I thought that if I had written and staged a play so obviously abounding in monstrous shortcomings, then I had lost all sensitivity and consequently my mechanism had run down once and for all."*

In fact, as Koni had tried to convince him, the failure was not Chekhov's. The premiere was a benefit performance for the

---

* *Anton Chekhov's Life and Thought: Selected Letters and Commentary*, edited and annotated by Simon Karlinsky, translated by Michael Henry Heim (Evanston, Illinois: Northwestern University Press, 1997), 284.

actress Elizaveta Levkeeva, known for playing in light comedies, and her admirers, who filled the theater on the opening night, were not expecting anything like what confronted them in *The Seagull*. The second and third performances, on the other hand, went very well. The brilliant young actress Vera Komissarzhevskaya, who played Nina Zarechnaya, wrote to Chekhov after the second night: "I've just returned from the theater, dear Anton Pavlovich . . . The play is a complete, unanimous success, just as it ought to be, just as it had to be. How I'd like to see you now, but what I'd like even more is for you to be present and hear the unanimous cry of 'Author.'"† Unfortunately, the reviews in the Petersburg press following the opening debacle were so bad that the theater management closed the show after only five performances.

The Seagull did not simply fly away, however. Over the next two years, the play was staged quite successfully in some twenty-one cities across Russia, the Ukraine and Georgia, and was also translated into Czech for a production in Prague. Meanwhile, during that same time, an event of great importance for Russian and world theater was taking place: Vladimir Nemirovich-Danchenko, a playwright and director, and the actor-director-theorist Konstantin Stanislavsky were in the process of founding a new theater dedicated to the highest professional quality—the Moscow Art Theatre. The two men met for the first time on June 22, 1897, over lunch at the Slavyansky Bazar hotel in Moscow. They sat down at two P.M. and talked until eight A.M. the next morning, ending with a fully formed project for their theater: Nemirovich-Danchenko would be in charge of repertory and literary matters in general, Stanislavsky in charge of production, and they would both direct. Next they had to choose the actors and plays for their first season, which was planned for the winter of 1898.

Chekhov was born in 1860. Stanislavsky was three years younger, Nemirovich two years older. They were both familiar with Chekhov's work, and in particular with his two four-act plays, *Ivanov* and *The Wood Demon*, which had been staged in Moscow in

† *Ibid.*, 283.

1887 and 1889. Nemirovich had known and been in correspondence with Chekhov since 1888, and had strongly disagreed with the negative reviews of *The Seagull*. On April 25, 1898, he wrote to him asking for permission to include the play in the opening season of the newly founded theater. Chekhov was on his way back to Russia from the south of France and received the letter only on May 6. On May 16 he wrote giving Nemirovich rights to stage not only *The Seagull* but his other plays as well. That October *The Seagull* went into rehearsal, with its opening set for December 17. Stanislavsky himself was to play the writer Trigorin; the young Vsevolod Meyerhold, who would become a famous director and innovator in his own right, took the part of Konstantin Treplyov; and the role of the actress Arkadina went to Olga Knipper, who three years later became Chekhov's wife.

The plays in that first season included *Tsar Fyodor Ioannovych* by Alexei K. Tolstoy, *The Sunken Bell* by Gerhart Hauptmann, the *Antigone* of Sophocles, Shakespeare's *The Merchant of Venice* and Goldoni's *La Locandiera*. *Tsar Fyodor Ioannovych*, which opened the season, was very well received by both audience and press, but the others had a cooler reception, and there was great tension in the dressing rooms on the opening night of *The Seagull*. In his memoirs, *My Life in the Russian Theatre*, Nemirovich recorded the moment that followed the first act:

> There was a silence, a complete silence both in the theater and on the stage, it was as though all held their breath, as though no one quite understood [what they had seen] . . . This mood lasted quite a long time, so long indeed that those onstage decided that the first act had failed, failed so completely that not a single friend in the audience dared applaud . . . Then suddenly, in the auditorium something happened. It was as if a dam had burst, or a bomb had exploded—all at once there was a deafening crash of applause from all: from friends and enemies.[‡]

‡ Quoted in *Chekhov, Four Plays and Three Jokes*, introduction and translation by Sharon Marie Carnicke (Indianapolis and Cambridge: Hackett, 2009), xxxi.

Chekhov had attended some earlier rehearsals, but avoided the opening; he distracted himself with his new house in Yalta. Nemirovich sent him a telegram shortly after midnight on December 18:

> Just finished playing *The Seagull*, colossal success. After the first act such applause that a series of triumphs followed. At my statement after the third act that the author was not present the audience demanded a telegram be sent to you on their behalf. We are all delirious with joy. We all embrace you, will write in detail.[§]

A new era in Russian theater had begun. Its emblem was the stylized image of a seagull that was sewn onto the Art Theatre's curtain. It is there to this day.

. . .

In a letter to his friend and publisher Alexei Suvorin, on October 21, 1895, Chekhov announced: ". . . I'm writing a play . . . not without pleasure, though I'm violating the conventions of the stage quite terribly. A comedy, three women's parts, six men's, four acts, landscapes (view of a lake); much talk about literature, little action, five tons of love."

Chekhov's practice of "violating the conventions of the stage" puzzled Tolstoy, who once asked him about *Uncle Vanya*: "What's it all about? Where's the drama?" In fact, the subtitle of *The Seagull*, "A Comedy in Four Acts," already begs the question. It is certainly not a comedy in any conventional sense. Calling it a comedy may have been something of a provocation on Chekhov's part, aimed at directors and actors. He wanted a different manner of playing than in the melodramas of the day; he wanted it to be light and quick; he wanted an internal shifting of tones rather than a single overarch-

§ *The Moscow Art Theatre Letters*, edited and translated by Jean Benedetti (London: Routledge, 1991), 42.

ing effect. Comedy flashes repeatedly in the exchanges between his characters, and disappears again. The aim is not laughter *per se*. It is also not satire, though there are sharply satirical moments in the play. It is a serious comedy of human contradictions.

There is no central idea in *The Seagull*, nor in any of Chekhov's last plays; there is no social message, no final revelation, apparently no unifying vision. Separate people go their separate ways. They seem to walk past each other and talk past each other; they keep repeating the same words, harping on the same obsessions. "One of Chekhov's most important innovations," Harvey Pitcher wrote in *The Chekhov Play*, "was to decentralize his cast. The traditional idea of hero and heroine has been discarded. No single character is allowed to stand out as more central than any other . . ."¶ This quality of Chekhov's dramaturgy happened to suit the notions of the new Moscow Art Theatre, with its stress on the ensemble over individual stars (in Stanislavsky's famous phrase, "There are no small parts, only small actors"). But for Chekhov it was not simply a technical innovation. Here is Sorin's country estate with its view of the lake; and here is this odd conglomeration of people, with their disagreements about literature and theater, with their "five tons of love"—a love that separates them more than it unites them. Their active lives are over (Sorin, Dorn), or not yet begun (Treplyov, Nina), or go on elsewhere (Arkadina, Trigorin). There is indeed "little action" in the play itself. The few dramatic events happen offstage. What unites the characters is not their involvement in a well-constructed plot; it is their happening to be together in a place suspended in time. There is no hierarchy among them; they are one in their exposed humanity. Chekhov's portrayal of them is both humorous and pitiless.

In 1892 Chekhov bought the small country estate of Melikhovo, some fifty miles south of Moscow. He settled in with his parents, his sister, and his younger brother in March and lived there more or less permanently until 1899, when he moved to Yalta. It

¶ *The Chekhov Play*, by Harvey Pitcher (Berkeley and London: University of California Press, 1985), 13.

was a one-story house, with a garden and a view not of a lake but of a very small pond. Chekhov wrote *The Seagull* and *Uncle Vanya* there, along with some of his finest stories. He also cultivated the garden, planted trees, served as a doctor in free clinics for the local peasants (there were cholera epidemics in 1892 and 1893), and built three schools in Melikhovo and neighboring villages, which he also supplied with furniture and textbooks. His life there bore little resemblance to the suspended life on Sorin's estate.

Yet Melikhovo plays an important role in *The Seagull*. Chekhov invited friends, writers, artists, actors to visit him, among them the novelist and playwright Ignaty Potapenko, the painter Isaac Levitan, and several women, writers or performers, who were more or less in love with him. Details of their collective life on the estate turned up in the play. In 1895, Levitan, who was a very close friend, tried to shoot himself over an affair with a woman. He ended up with a slight wound and a white bandage on his head. Potapenko, who was married, seduced the young opera singer Lydia Mizinova, whom he met at Melikhovo and who had been hopelessly in love with Chekhov. Potapenko took her away to Paris, and, when she became pregnant, abandoned her and went back to his wife. On reading the manuscript of *The Seagull*, which Chekhov, perhaps maliciously, entrusted to him for copying and passing on to the censors, he could hardly help recognizing himself in the character of Trigorin. Another guest at Melikhovo, the writer Lydia Avilova, once gave Chekhov a medallion inscribed with a reference to a line from one of his own stories: "If you ever need my life, come and take it." The same line, now attributed to one of Trigorin's stories, is referred to on the medallion that Nina gives to the writer toward the end of Act Three. What's more, Chekhov actually gave Avilova's medallion to the actress who played Nina. Even the complaining, underpaid schoolteacher Medvedenko had his prototype in a teacher from one of the local schools near Melikhovo. And Chekhov's guests, like Arkadina's, used to gather and play lotto in the evenings.

How does Chekhov bring the realia, or banalia, of life at Melikhovo onstage in *The Seagull*? How does the stage transform them, when they are held up as an image? The play opens with a play within the play, Treplyov's symbolist ("decadent," as his mother says) experiment with "new forms." It immediately invites comparison with what we are actually watching, that is, with Chekhov's supposed naturalism. Treplyov's play is abstract, peopleless: "A curtain, then the wings, then empty space. No scenery." So Treplyov describes it. It is the opposite of Stanislavsky's staging, which is filled with details of everyday life, trees, bushes, lawns, benches, chairs, tables, draperies, lamps, the sounds of wind and rain, the barking of a dog, the croaking of frogs. There are still some traces of older theater—Trigorin's long monologue in Act Two, a few brief soliloquies. But his characters never play to the audience or acknowledge its existence. On the contrary, they keep to their separate world. In Act One they even turn their backs to the audience as they watch Treplyov's play. And at the end of Act Three the stage is left empty; we hear the noises of departure from outside, people saying good-bye; a maid rushes in, picks up a forgotten basket of plums, and rushes out again, as if nobody was looking.

It is all very real, ordinary, nothing like the parodied symbolism of Treplyov's play, and yet it has its own symbolic resonance. The most obvious symbol in the play is the seagull of the title. Early in Act One, Nina tells Treplyov: "It's the lake that draws me here, like a seagull . . ." In Act Two, Treplyov enters and presents Nina with a seagull that he has shot. "Soon I'll kill myself the same way," he tells her rather melodramatically, to which she replies: ". . . you express yourself incomprehensibly, in symbols of some kind. And this seagull is also apparently a symbol, but, forgive me, I don't understand . . . I'm too simple to understand you." Later in the same act, Trigorin enters, sees the dead seagull, and immediately jots down an idea for a story, which he tells to Nina, and which nearly becomes the story of their relationship. In Act Four, two years later, Treplyov tells Dorn he has been receiving letters from Nina, which she signs "Seagull." In her last scene with him, she keeps saying "I'm the seagull," meaning, as she alone knows, the seagull of Trigorin's story. But she finally rejects the identification and goes off to live her own unsymbolic life. And when Trigorin is presented with the same seagull, now stuffed, in the last moments of the play, he cannot remember anything about it.

There is a more subtle symbolism in the changing sets of the four acts. The space gradually shrinks: in Act One there is the open space of the park and the wide alley; in Act Two the house appears far upstage right; in Act Three they move inside to the dining room, and in Act Four to the cluttered drawing room, which Treplyov has turned into a study, and which is being made up as we watch into a bedroom for the ailing Sorin—meaning that it is virtually the only inhabited room in the house. There are doors to other rooms on either side and a glass door straight ahead leading to the terrace. Toward the end of the act, Treplyov locks one of the side doors and barricades the other. He is alone there with Nina for their last scene together. She comes in through the glass door, and in the end she walks out again through the same glass door. Her future is open. But Treplyov can no longer pass through the door, transparent though it is. The denouement occurs moments later, offstage.

—*Richard Pevear*

A NOTE ON THE TRANSLATION

In our translation of *The Seagull*, we include a number of lines from the 1896 copy of the play (sent to the censor for approval of the premiere production in St. Petersburg), which do not appear in the script for the Moscow Art Theatre 1898 revival, nor in subsequent translations of the play.

The variants we include fall into three categories:

First, there are simple additions throughout the play, which may help future directors discover a richer, even deeper understanding of the play and its characters, as well as of Chekhov's intentions. For example, we have reinstated Masha's line at the beginning of Act Two: "Mamma brought me up like that fairy-tale girl who lived in a flower. I don't know how to do anything." I think this offers an insight into Masha's character and certainly into her background and the life she has lived on the estate. We separate these "restored" lines from the canonical text with brackets.

Second, we suggest one small cut. In Act Three, after Arkadina has wooed back Trigorin, she has an aside: "*(To herself)* Now he's mine" (see page 65). This line does not appear in the 1896 script of the play; it was added later, perhaps for the Moscow Art production, perhaps even during their rehearsals. It strikes me as a very odd addition, as it is certainly more melodramatic than anything else in the play or in any of Chekhov's other mature plays.

Third, in Act Four there is an alternative scenario, which includes different (and additional) lines and stage directions. They concern Sorin. In the canonical version, Sorin, in his wheelchair, is taken off to dinner and never returns. This has always seemed very odd to me, as until this point, Sorin, with his worsening illness, has been the entire reason for the gathering. So it seems strange that he is then forgotten for the rest of the play. In the earlier 1896 version, Sorin is not forgotten. In fact, he remains onstage, asleep, throughout the entire Treplyov/Nina scene and then for the rest of the play. There are lines and stage directions which reflect this. We have included both the canonical and this earlier interesting variation, also in brackets.

—Richard Nelson

THE SEAGULL

Characters

IRÍNA NIKOLÁEVNA ARKÁDINA, an actress

KONSTANTÍN GAVRÍLYCH TREPLYÓV, her son, an aspiring writer

PYÓTR NIKOLÁICH SÓRIN, her brother, a retired state councillor

NÍNA MIKHÁILOVNA ZARÉCHNAYA, a young girl, daughter of a local
   landowner

ILYÁ AFANÁSYICH SHAMRÁEV, a retired lieutenant, Sorin's steward

POLÍNA ANDRÉEVNA, his wife

MÁSHA, their daughter

BORÍS ALEXÉICH TRIGÓRIN, a successful writer

EVGÉNY SERGÉICH DORN, a doctor

SEMYÓN SEMYÓNYCH MEDVEDÉNKO, a teacher

YÁKOV, a workman

COOK

MAID

The action takes place on Sorin's estate. Two years pass between
Acts Three and Four.

ACT ONE

Part of the park on Sorin's estate. A wide alley leading into the park from the audience toward the lake is obstructed by a stage, hastily knocked together for an amateur performance, so that the lake cannot be seen. Bushes to the left and right of the stage.

Several chairs, a little table.

The sun has just set. On the stage, behind the closed curtain, Yakov and other workmen; sounds of coughing and hammering. Masha and Medvedenko enter left, returning from a stroll.

MEDVEDENKO

Why do you always go around in black?

MASHA

It's in mourning for my life.[1] I'm unhappy.

MEDVEDENKO

Why? *(Reflecting)* I don't understand . . . You're in good health, your father may not be rich but he's well-off. My life is much harder than yours. I get only twenty-three rubles a month, minus pension deductions, but I don't wear mourning.

They sit down.

MASHA

The point isn't money. A poor man can be happy, too.

MEDVEDENKO

That's in theory, but in practice it turns out like this: me, my mother, my sisters, and my little brother, and my salary's all of twenty-three rubles. We've got to eat and drink, haven't we? Need tea and sugar? Tobacco? That keeps you juggling.

MASHA

(Looking at the stage) The play will begin soon.

MEDVEDENKO

Yes. Miss Zarechnaya's acting, and the play is by Konstantin Gavrilych. They're in love, and today their souls will merge in striving to form one single artistic image. But my soul and yours have no common points of contact. I love you, my longing will not let me stay home, every day I walk four miles here and four miles back, and I only meet with phlegmatism on your part. That's understandable. I'm without means, I have a big family . . . Who wants to marry a man who has nothing to eat himself?

MASHA

Nonsense. *(Takes snuff)* Your love touches me, I just can't reciprocate, that's all. *(Offers him the snuffbox)* Help yourself.

MEDVEDENKO

I don't feel like it.

Pause.

MASHA

It's stifling. There'll probably be a thunderstorm tonight. You keep philosophizing or talking about money. In your opinion there's no greater misfortune than poverty, but in my opinion it's a thousand times easier to go around in rags and beg, than . . . Anyhow, you won't understand that . . .

Sorin and Treplyov enter from right.

SORIN

(Leaning on a cane) I somehow feel out of sorts in the country, my boy, and, needless to say, I'll never get used to it here. Last night I went to bed at ten, and this morning I woke up at nine feeling as if my brain got stuck to my skull from sleeping so long and all that. *(Laughs)* And after lunch I accidentally fell asleep again, and now I'm a total wreck—it's a nightmare, finally . . .

TREPLYOV

Right, you ought to live in town. *(Seeing Masha and Medvedenko)* Wait, we'll call you when it starts, but you mustn't be here now. Go away, please.

SORIN

(To Masha) Marya Ilyinichna, kindly ask your father to order the dog untied, otherwise he howls. My sister couldn't sleep all night again.

[MASHA

Tell him yourself. There's millet in the barn now, and he says without the dog thieves will get it.

TREPLYOV

To hell with the millet.]

MASHA

You speak to my father, I'm not going to. Spare me that, please. *(To Medvedenko)* Let's go!

MEDVEDENKO

(To Treplyov) So let us know before it begins.

They both exit.

SORIN

That means the dog will howl all night again. It's funny, I've never lived in the country the way I wanted. I used to take a month's vacation and come here to get some rest and all that, but they'd pester you so much with millet and oats that you'd already want to clear out on the first day. *(Laughs)* I always found it a pleasure to leave this place . . . Well, now I'm retired and I've got nowhere to go, finally. Live here, like it or not . . .

YAKOV

(To Treplyov) We're going for a swim, Konstantin Gavrilych.

TREPLYOV

All right. Only be back in your places in ten minutes. *(Looks at his watch)* We'll start soon.

YAKOV

Yes, sir. *(Exits)*

TREPLYOV

(Looking at the stage) There's a theater for you. A curtain, then the wings, then empty space. No scenery. The view opens straight onto the lake and the horizon. We'll raise the curtain at exactly eight thirty, when the moon rises.

SORIN

Splendid.

TREPLYOV

If Miss Zarechnaya is late, then of course the whole effect is lost. It's time she was here. Her father and stepmother keep a close eye on her, and escaping from home is as hard for her as escaping from prison. *(Straightens his uncle's necktie)* Your hair and beard are a mess. You ought to get a trim, or something . . .

SORIN

(Combing his beard) The tragedy of my life. Even when I was young, I looked like a heavy boozer—and all that. Women never liked me. *(Sitting down)* Why is my sister in a bad mood?

TREPLYOV

Why? She's bored. *(Sitting down beside him)* She's jealous. She's already against me, and against the performance, and against my play, because her novelist might like Miss Zarechnaya. She doesn't know my play, but she already hates it.

SORIN

(Laughs) That's all in your head, really . . .

TREPLYOV

It annoys her that it's Miss Zarechnaya and not she who's to have a success on this little stage. *(After glancing at his watch)* She's a curious case psychologically—my mother. Unquestionably talented, intelligent, capable of weeping over a book, she'll reel off all Nekrasov for you by heart, she looks after sick people like an angel; but try praising Duse in her presence. Oh-ho! You have to praise only her alone, you have to write about her, cheer, go into raptures over her acting in *La dame aux camélias* or *The Fumes of Life*,[2] but here in the country there's none of that drug, so she gets bored and ill-tempered, and we're all her enemies, we're all to blame. What's more, she's superstitious, she's afraid of three candles, of the number thirteen. She's stingy. She's got seventy thousand in a bank in Odessa—I know that for sure. But ask her for a loan, she bursts into tears.

SORIN

You've imagined that your mother doesn't like your play, and you're worked up and all that. Don't worry, your mother adores you.

TREPLYOV

(Tearing petals from a flower) She loves me, she loves me not; she loves me, she loves me not; she loves me, she loves me not. *(Laughs)* See, my mother loves me not. Of course! She wants to live, to love, to wear bright-colored blouses, but I'm already twenty-five, and I'm a constant reminder to her that she's not young anymore. When I'm not there, she's only thirty-two, but when I'm around she's forty-three, and she hates me for that. She also knows that I don't accept her theater. She loves theater, it seems to her that she's serving mankind, sacred art, but in my opinion contemporary theater is in a rut, the same old notions. When the curtain rises and in the evening light, in a room with three walls, these great talents, these priests of sacred art portray how people eat, drink, love, walk, wear their jackets; when they try to fish a moral from trite scenes and phrases—a small, easily understandable moral, suitable for domestic use; when I'm offered a thousand variations on the same thing, the same thing, the same thing—I flee, I flee, as Maupassant fled from the Eiffel Tower, which oppressed his brain with its triteness.[3]

SORIN

But we can't do without theater.

TREPLYOV

There's a need for new forms. New forms are needed, and if there aren't any, then better nothing. *(Looks at his watch)* I love my mother, I love her very much, but she leads a disorderly life, constantly fusses with that writer, [but she smokes, drinks, lives openly with that novelist,] her name keeps getting dragged into the papers—and that wears me out. Sometimes it's simple selfishness speaking; I'm sorry my mother is a well-known actress, and it seems if she had been an ordinary woman, I would be happier. Tell me, uncle, how could there be a more desperate and stupid situation: there sit her guests, all of them celebrities, actors and writers, and among them I alone am nothing, and they tolerate me only because I'm her son. Who am I? What am I? I left the university in my third year for reasons "beyond our control," as publishers say, no talents, not a drop of money, and according to my passport I'm a Kiev tradesman. My father was a Kiev tradesman, though he, too, was a well-known actor. And so, when all these actors and writers in her drawing room happened to turn their gracious attention to me, it seemed to me that their eyes were measuring my insignificance—I guessed their thoughts and suffered from the humiliation . . .

SORIN

By the way, tell me, please, what sort of man is her novelist? I can't figure him out. He never says anything.

TREPLYOV

He's an intelligent man, simple, slightly—you know—melancholy. Very respectable. He won't turn forty for a while yet, but he's already famous and fed up, fed up . . . [Now he only drinks beer, and is only able to love women who are no longer young.] As for his writing, it's . . . how shall I put it? Nice, talented . . . but . . . after Tolstoy or Zola you don't want to read Trigorin.

SORIN

Well, I like men of letters, my boy. Once upon a time I passionately wanted two things: to get married and to be a man of letters. But I didn't manage either. Yes. Even being a minor man of letters would be good enough, finally.

TREPLYOV

(Listens) I hear footsteps . . . *(Embraces his uncle)* I can't live without her . . . Even the sound of her footsteps is beautiful . . . I'm insanely happy. *(Quickly goes to meet Nina as she enters)* My magic! My dream . . .

NINA

(Agitated) I'm not late . . . I'm sure I'm not late . . .

TREPLYOV

(Kissing her hands) No, no, no . . .

NINA

I've been worrying all day, I was so scared! I was afraid father wouldn't let me . . . But he's just left with my stepmother. The sky's red, the moon's beginning to rise, and I drove my horse hard, really hard. *(Laughs)* But I'm glad. *(Presses Sorin's hand firmly)*

SORIN

(Laughs) You seem to have tears in your pretty little eyes . . . Heh-heh! Naughty!

NINA

It's just . . . Look how out of breath I am. I'll leave in half an hour, we must hurry. No, no, for God's sake, don't try to keep me. Father doesn't know I'm here.

TREPLYOV

In fact, it's time we started. Someone go and call everybody.

SORIN

I'll go and all that. This minute. *(Goes off right and sings)* "To France two grenadiers . . ."[4] *(Turns around)* I once started singing like that, and some assistant prosecutor says to me: "You've got a powerful voice, Your Excellency . . . " Then he thought a bit and said: "Powerful . . . but repulsive." *(Laughs and exits)*

NINA

Father and his wife don't let me come here. They say its bohemian . . . they're afraid I'll become an actress . . . But it's the lake that draws me here, like a seagull . . . My heart is full of you. *(Looks around)*

TREPLYOV

We're alone.

NINA

I think somebody's there . . .

TREPLYOV

Nobody. *(They kiss)*

NINA

What kind of tree is this?

TREPLYOV

An elm.

NINA

Why does it look so dark?

TREPLYOV

It's already evening, all things turn dark. Don't leave early, I beg you.

NINA

I can't stay.

TREPLYOV

What if I go to your place, Nina? I'll stand all night in the garden and look at your window.

NINA

You mustn't, the watchman will see you. Trésor isn't used to you yet and he'll bark.

TREPLYOV

I love you.

NINA

Shh . . .

TREPLYOV

(Hears footsteps) Who's there? Is it you, Yakov?

YAKOV

(Behind the stage) Yes, sir.

TREPLYOV

Take your places. It's time. Is the moon rising?

YAKOV

Yes, sir.

TREPLYOV

You've got the alcohol? The sulfur? When the red eyes appear, there should be a smell of sulfur. *(To Nina)* Go, everything's ready there. Are you nervous? . . .

NINA

Yes, very. Never mind your mother, I'm not afraid of her, but Trigorin's here . . . I'm scared and embarrassed to act in front of him . . . A well-known writer . . . Is he young?

TREPLYOV

Yes.

NINA

His stories are so wonderful!

TREPLYOV

(Coldly) I don't know, I haven't read them.

NINA

It's hard to act in your play. There are no living people in it.

TREPLYOV

Living people! Life must be portrayed not as it is, and not as it ought to be, but as it comes to us in dreams.

NINA

There's not much action in your play, just reciting. And in my opinion there simply must be love in a play . . .

They exit behind the stage. Enter Polina Andreevna and Dorn.

POLINA ANDREEVNA

It's getting damp. Go back, put on your galoshes.

DORN

I'm hot.

POLINA ANDREEVNA

You don't take care of yourself. It's pigheadedness. You're a doctor and you know perfectly well that damp air is bad for you, but you want me to suffer. Yesterday you deliberately sat out all evening on the terrace . . .

DORN

(Sings to himself) "Say not your youth was ruined . . ."[5]

POLINA ANDREEVNA

You got so carried away talking with Irina Nikolaevna . . . you didn't notice the cold. Admit you like her . . .

DORN

I'm fifty-five.

POLINA ANDREEVNA

Nonsense, for a man that's not old. You're in fine shape and women still find you attractive.

DORN

So what can I do for you?

POLINA ANDREEVNA

You men are always ready to fall on your faces in front of an actress. All of you!

DORN

(Sings to himself) "Again I stand before thee . . ."[6] If society likes actors and treats them differently than, say, merchants, that's in the order of things. It's called idealism.

POLINA ANDREEVNA

Women have always fallen in love with you and hung on your neck. Is that also idealism?

DORN

(Shrugging) Well, so what? There was a lot of good in the way women related to me. They mainly liked the excellent doctor in me. Ten or fifteen years ago, remember, I was the only decent obstetrician in the whole province. And I've always been an honorable man.

POLINA ANDREEVNA

(Seizing him by the hand) My dearest!

DORN

Quiet. They're coming.

Enter Arkadina on Sorin's arm, Trigorin, Shamraev, Medvedenko and Masha.

SHAMRAEV

In the year eighteen hundred and seventy-three, at the fair in Poltava, she acted magnificently. Sheer ecstasy! She acted amazingly! And would you happen to know what's become of the comic actor Pavel Semyonych Chadin? He was inimitable as Raspluev, better than Sadovsky, I swear to you, my most esteemed lady.[7] What's become of him?

ARKADINA

You keep asking about some sort of antediluvians. How should I know! *(Sits down)*

SHAMRAEV

(With a sigh) Dear old Pashka Chadin! There's none like him today. The stage has declined, Irina Nikolaevna! There used to be sturdy oaks, but now all we see is stumps.

DORN

There are few brilliant talents, it's true, but the average actor has become better.

SHAMRAEV

I cannot agree with you. However, it's a matter of taste. *De gustibus aut bene, aut nihil.*[8]

Treplyov enters from behind the stage.

[MASHA

(Offers Trigorin her snuffbox) Help yourself. Are you always so silent, or do you speak sometimes?

TRIGORIN

Yes, I do speak sometimes. *(Takes snuff)* Revolting! How can you!

MASHA

You have a kind smile. You must be a simple man.]

ARKADINA

(To her son) My dear son, when will it begin?

TREPLYOV

In a minute. Please be patient.

15

ARKADINA

(Quotes from Hamlet*:)*

My son!
Thou turn'st mine eyes into my very soul;
And there I see such black and grained spots
As will not leave their tinct.

TREPLYOV

(From Hamlet*:)*

Nay, but to live
In the rank sweat of an enseamed bed,
Stew'd in corruption, honeying and making love
Over the nasty sty.[9]

A horn sounds from behind the stage.

Ladies and gentlemen, the beginning! Attention, please!

Pause.

I begin. *(He taps a stick and says loudly)* O you venerable old shades, who hover over the lake at nighttime, put us to sleep, and let us dream what will be two hundred thousand years from now!

SORIN

Two hundred thousand years from now there'll be nothing at all.

TREPLYOV

Then let this nothing be portrayed.

ARKADINA

Yes, let it. We're asleep.

The curtain opens, revealing the view of the lake; the moon is on the horizon, its reflection in the water; on a big stone sits Nina, all in white.

NINA

People, lions, eagles and partridges, antlered deer, geese, spiders,
silent fish inhabiting the waters, starfish and those not visible to
the eye—in short, all living things, all living things, all living things
have completed their sad round and are extinct . . . For thousands
of years already the earth has not borne upon itself a single living
being, and this poor moon lights its lamp in vain. The cranes no
longer awaken with a cry in the meadows, nor are the june bugs
heard in the linden groves. Cold, cold, cold. Empty, empty, empty.
Eerie, eerie, eerie.

Pause.

The bodies of living beings have vanished into dust, and eternal
matter has turned them into stone, into water, into cloud, and their
souls have all merged into one. I . . . I . . . am that universal soul of
the world. In me is the soul of Alexander the Great, and Caesar,
and Shakespeare, and Napoleon, and the merest leech. In me the
consciousness of men has merged with the instinct of animals, and
I remember all, all, all, and in myself I relive each life anew.

Will-o'-the-wisps appear.

ARKADINA

(Softly) This is like the Decadents.

TREPLYOV

(Pleadingly and with reproach) Mama!

NINA

I am alone. Once every hundred years I part my lips to speak, and
my voice sounds mournful in this emptiness, and no one hears me
. . . And you, pale fires, do not hear me . . . The putrid marsh gives
birth to you towards morning, and you wander till dawn, but without thought, without will, without the tremor of life. Fearing lest
life emerge in you, the devil, father of eternal matter, brings about

in you a continuous exchange of atoms, as in stones and water, and you change ceaselessly. The spirit alone remains constant and unchanging in the universe.

Pause.

Like a prisoner cast into a deep empty well, I do not know where I am or what awaits me. The only thing not concealed from me is that in a cruel, unrelenting struggle with the devil, the source of all material powers, I am destined to be victorious, after which matter and spirit will merge in beautiful harmony and the kingdom of universal will shall come. But that will only come about when little by little, over a long, long series of millennia, the moon, and bright Sirius, and the earth turn to dust . . . And until then horror, horror . . .

Pause. Two red dots appear against the background of the lake.

Here my powerful adversary, the devil, approaches. I see his frightful crimson eyes.

ARKADINA

There's a smell of sulfur. Is that part of it?

TREPLYOV

Yes.

ARKADINA

(Laughs) Right, a special effect.

TREPLYOV

Mama!

NINA

He's bored without man . . .

POLINA ANDREEVNA

(To Dorn) You've taken your hat off. Put it on, or you'll catch cold.

ARKADINA

The doctor took his hat off to the devil, the father of eternal matter.

TREPLYOV

(Flaring up) The play's over! Enough! Curtain!

ARKADINA

Why are you angry?

TREPLYOV

Enough! Curtain! Close the curtain! *(Stamping his foot)* Curtain!

The curtain is closed.

Sorry! I lost sight of the fact that only a few chosen ones can write plays and act on the stage. I violated the monopoly! For me . . . I . . . *(Wants to say more, but waves his hand and exits left)*

ARKADINA

What's got into him?

SORIN

Irina, old girl, you mustn't treat youthful vanity like that.

ARKADINA

What did I say?

SORIN

You offended him.

ARKADINA

He said himself that it was a joke, so I treated his play as a joke.

SORIN

But still . . .

ARKADINA

Now it turns out that he's written a great work! Imagine that! It means he set up this performance and wafted sulfur at us not as a joke, but to make a point . . . He wanted to teach us how to write and what to perform. It gets boring in the end. These constant sallies against me and these barbs—say what you like, they're tiresome! Capricious, egotistical boy.

SORIN

He wanted to please you.

ARKADINA

Oh? Yet he didn't pick some ordinary sort of play, but forced us to listen to this decadent raving. I'm even ready to listen to raving for the sake of a joke, but these are pretenses to new forms, to a new era in art. And I don't think there are any new forms here, but simply bad character.

TRIGORIN

Each of us writes as he wants and as he can.

ARKADINA

Let him write as he wants and as he can, only let him leave me in peace.

DORN

Thou art angry, Jupiter . . . [10]

ARKADINA

I'm not Jupiter, I'm a woman. *(Lights a cigarette)* I'm not angry, I'm just annoyed that a young man can be so boring. I didn't mean to offend him.

[NINA

(Peeks out from behind the curtain) Is this the end? We won't continue?

ARKADINA

The author left. It must be the end. Come out to us, sweetheart.

NINA

Just a moment. *(Disappears)*

MEDVEDENKO

(To Masha) All this depends on the essence of psychic substance.] No one has any grounds for separating spirit from matter, since it may be that spirit itself is a combination of material atoms. *(Animatedly, to Trigorin)* You know what, why not describe the life of us schoolteachers in a play and perform that onstage. A hard, hard life!

ARKADINA

Fair enough, but let's not talk about plays or atoms. What a fine evening! Do you hear that singing? *(Listens)* How nice!

POLINA ANDREEVNA

It's from the other side.

Pause.

ARKADINA

(To Trigorin) Sit beside me. Ten or fifteen years ago, here, on the lake, you could hear music and singing constantly almost every night. There are six country estates here on the shore. I remember laughter, noise, shotguns, and romances, romances all the time . . . Back then the *jeune premier*[11] and idol of all these six estates was— allow me to introduce *(Nods to Dorn)* Doctor Evgeny Sergeich. He's charming even now, but then he was irresistible.

[*Polina Andreevna quietly weeps.*

SHAMRAEV

(Reproachfully) Polina, Polina . . .

POLINA ANDREEVNA

Never mind. Sorry. I suddenly felt so sad!]

ARKADINA

Ah, my conscience is beginning to trouble me. Why did I offend my poor boy? I'm worried now. *(Loudly)* Kostya! My son! Kostya!

MASHA

I'll go and look for him.

ARKADINA

Please do, my dear.

MASHA

(Goes toward left) Halloo! Konstantin Gavrilych! . . . Halloo! *(Exits)*

NINA

(Entering from behind the stage) Obviously we won't continue, so I can come out. Hello! *(Exchanges kisses with Arkadina and Polina Andreevna)*

SORIN

Bravo! Bravo!

ARKADINA

Bravo! Bravo! We all admired you. With such looks, with such a wonderful voice, you mustn't sit here in the country, it's sinful. You certainly have talent. Do you hear? You really must go on the stage!

NINA

Oh, that's my dream! *(Sighing)* But it will never come true.

ARKADINA

Who knows? Here, let me introduce you: Boris Alexeich Trigorin.

NINA

Ah, I'm so glad . . . *(Embarrassed)* I read you all the time . . .

ARKADINA

(Seating her beside him) Don't be embarrassed, dear. He's famous, but he has a simple soul. See, he's embarrassed himself.

DORN

I guess we can open the curtain now. It feels spooky.

SHAMRAEV

(Loudly) Yakov, open the curtain!

The curtain opens.

NINA

(To Trigorin) A strange play, isn't it?

TRIGORIN

I didn't understand a thing. But it was a pleasure to watch. You acted with such sincerity. And the set was beautiful.

Pause.

There must be a lot of fish in this lake.

NINA

Yes.

[SHAMRAEV

Bream and pike, mostly. There are some perch, but not many.]

TRIGORIN

I like fishing. For me there's no greater pleasure than sitting on the shore in the evening and watching the bobber.

NINA

But I think, for someone who has experienced the pleasure of creative work, other pleasures no longer exist.

ARKADINA

(Laughing) Don't talk like that. When people say nice things to him, he gets completely rattled.

SHAMRAEV

I remember, at the opera in Moscow once the famous Silva took a low C. And just then, as luck would have it, the bass from the cathedral choir was sitting in the gallery, and suddenly—imagine our utter amazement—we hear from the gallery: "Bravo, Silva!"—a whole octave lower . . . Like this: *(In a low bass)* "Bravo, Silva . . ." The theater just gasped.

Pause.

DORN

The angel of silence flew over.

NINA

Time for me to go. Good-bye.

ARKADINA

Where? Where so early? We won't let you.

NINA

Papa's expecting me.

ARKADINA

What a man, really . . . *(They kiss)* Well, nothing to be done. It's a pity, a pity to let you go.

NINA

If you only knew how hard it is for me to leave!

ARKADINA

Someone should see you home, my little one.

NINA

(Frightened) Oh, no, no!

SORIN

(Pleading with her) Stay!

NINA

I can't, Pyotr Nikolaich.

SORIN

Stay for just an hour and all that. No, really . . . [Sweet, good, kind—honestly, it's boring without you.]

NINA

(After thinking, through tears) Impossible! *(Shakes hands with him and quickly exits)*

ARKADINA

An unfortunate girl, actually. They say her late mother bequeathed her husband the whole of her enormous fortune, to the last kopeck, and now the girl has nothing, because her father has already bequeathed everything to his second wife. It's outrageous.

DORN

Yes, her dear papa is a perfect beast, to do him full justice.

SORIN

(Rubbing his chilled hands) Let's us go, too, my friends, it's getting damp. My legs hurt.

ARKADINA

They're like wooden legs—you can barely walk. Well, let's go, old and miserable man. *(Takes him under the arm)*

SHAMRAEV

(Offering his arm to his wife) Madame?

SORIN

I hear that dog's been howling again. *(To Shamraev)* Be a good fellow, Ilya Afanasyich, tell them to untie it.

SHAMRAEV

Impossible, Pyotr Nikolaich, I'm afraid thieves will get into the barn. I've got millet stored in it. *(To Medvedenko, who is walking beside him)* Yes, a whole octave lower: "Bravo, Silva!" And he wasn't a professional, just a choir singer.

MEDVEDENKO

And what is a choir singer's salary?

All exit, except for Dorn.

DORN

(Alone) I don't know, maybe I don't understand anything, or I've lost my mind, but I liked the play. There's something to it. When this young girl talked about being alone, and then when the devil's red eyes appeared, my hands shook with excitement. It's fresh, naive . . . Ah, I think that's him coming. I feel like saying a whole lot of nice things to him.

TREPLYOV

(Enters) Everybody's gone.

DORN

I'm here.

TREPLYOV

Mashenka's hunting for me all over the park. Insufferable creature.

DORN

Konstantin Gavrilych, I liked your play very much. It's somewhat strange, and I didn't hear the end, but still it makes a strong impression. You're a talented man, you should continue.

Treplyov presses his hand hard and embraces him impulsively.

Pah, you're so nervous! Tears in your eyes . . . What do I mean to say? You took your subject from the realm of abstract ideas. That's the right thing to do, because a work of art must always express some great thought. Only what's serious is beautiful. How pale you are!

TREPLYOV

So you say—continue?

DORN

Yes . . . But portray only what's important and eternal. You know, I've lived my life with variety and zest, I'm content, but if I happened to experience the uplift of spirit that an artist feels in the moment of creation, then I think I would despise my material husk and all that's inherent in that husk, and would soar up from the earth into the heights.

TREPLYOV

Excuse me, but where's Miss Zarechnaya?

DORN

And here's another thing. A work must have a clear, definite thought in it. You should know why you're writing. Otherwise, if you follow this picturesque road without a definite purpose, you'll get lost, and your talent will be the ruin of you.

TREPLYOV

(Impatiently) Where's Miss Zarechnaya?

DORN

She went home.

TREPLYOV

(In despair) What am I going to do? I want to see her . . . I've got to see her . . . I'll go . . .

Masha enters.

DORN

(To Treplyov) Calm down, my friend.

TREPLYOV

Still, I'll go. I have to go.

MASHA

Go home, Konstantin Gavrilych. Your mama's waiting for you. She's worried.

TREPLYOV

Tell her I've gone. And I beg you all to leave me alone! Leave me! Don't come after me!

[MASHA

On what? My father will tell you all the horses are busy.

TREPLYOV

(Angrily) He has no right! I don't interfere in anybody's life. Let them leave me alone!]

DORN

But, but, but, my dear boy . . . not like this . . . It's not nice.

TREPLYOV

(Through tears) Good-bye, doctor. Thank you . . . *(Exits)*

DORN

(With a sigh) Youth, youth!

MASHA

When there's nothing left to say, they say: "Youth, youth!" *(Takes snuff)*

DORN

(Takes her snuffbox and throws it in the bushes) That's disgusting! *(Pause)* They seem to be playing the piano inside. Let's go.

MASHA

Wait.

DORN

What is it?

MASHA

I want to tell you again. I want to talk . . . *(Agitated)* I don't love my father . . . but my heart is drawn to you. For some reason I feel with my whole soul that you are close to me . . . Help me. Help me, or I'll do something stupid, I'll make a mockery of my life, I'll ruin it . . . I can't go on . . .

DORN

What? Help you how?

MASHA

I suffer. Nobody, nobody knows of my suffering! *(Rests her head on his chest, says softly)* I love Konstantin.

DORN

Everyone's so nervous! So nervous! And so much love . . . Oh, bewitching lake! *(Tenderly)* But what can I do, my child? What? What?

Curtain.

ACT TWO

———

A croquet lawn. Far upstage right a house with a large terrace. To the left the lake can be seen, with sunshine reflected in it. Flowerbeds. Noon. Hot. To one side of the lawn, on a bench in the shade of an old linden, sit Arkadina, Dorn and Masha. Dorn has an open book on his lap.

ARKADINA

(To Masha) Let's stand up.

They both stand up.

Stand next to me. You're twenty-two years old, I'm almost twice that. Evgeny Sergeich, which of us looks more youthful?

DORN

You do, of course.

ARKADINA

So there, miss . . . And why? Because I work, I feel, I'm constantly busy, while you go on sitting in the same place, you don't live . . .

[MASHA

Mama brought me up like that fairy-tale girl who lived in a flower. I don't know how to do anything.]

ARKADINA

And I make it a rule not to look into the future. I never think about old age or death. Whatever comes will come.

MASHA

And I have a feeling as if I was born long, long ago; I drag my life behind me like an endless train on a dress. And often I have no wish to live. *(Sits down)* Of course, that's all nonsense. I must stir myself up, shake it all off.

DORN

(Singing softly) "Tell it to her, my flowers . . ."[12]

ARKADINA

I'm also proper as an Englishman. I keep myself neat as a pin, as they say, and I'm always dressed and have my hair done *comme il faut*. Would I allow myself to step out of the house, even just to this garden, in a housecoat or with my hair down? Never. I'm well preserved, because I've never been a slouch, never let myself go, as some do . . . *(Strolls about the lawn, arms akimbo)* There—see me strut. I could play a fifteen year old.

DORN

Well, ma'am, nevertheless I'll keep going. *(Picks up the book)* We stopped at the grain merchant and the rats . . .

ARKADINA

And the rats. Read. *(Sits down)* Or, no, give it to me, I'll read. It's my turn. *(Takes the book and looks for the place)* And the rats . . .

Here it is . . . *(Reads)* "And, to be sure, for society people to pamper novelists and invite them into their homes is as dangerous as for grain merchants to breed rats in their barns. Yet they are loved. And so, when a woman has selected a writer whom she wishes to captivate, she besieges him with compliments, courtesies and indulgences . . ."[13] Well, that's true of the French, maybe, but with us there's nothing like that, no such strategies. With us, if you want to know, before she captivates a writer, a woman is already head over heels in love with him. Don't look far, take me and Trigorin . . . [I didn't select Boris Alexeich, didn't captivate him, but when I met him everything in my head turned upside down, and, my dear hearts, I felt faint. I used to stand and look at him and cry. You see, I'd howl and howl. What kind of strategy is that?]

Enter Sorin, leaning on a cane, and beside him, Nina; Medvedenko is rolling an empty wheelchair after them.

SORIN

(The way one fusses over children) So? We're pleased? We're finally feeling cheerful? *(To his sister)* We're pleased! Our father and stepmother have gone to Tver, and we're free now for a whole three days.

NINA

(Sits down beside Arkadina and embraces her) I'm happy. I belong to you now.

SORIN

(Sits down in his wheelchair) She's a pretty little thing today.

ARKADINA

Dressed up, attractive . . . That shows you're a smart girl. *(Kisses Nina)* But we mustn't praise you too much or it will be bad luck. Where's Boris Alexeich?

NINA

He's down by the bathhouse fishing.

ARKADINA

Isn't he sick of it? *(Wants to go on reading)*

NINA

What's that?

ARKADINA

Maupassant's *On the Water*, sweetie.

[MEDVEDENKO

Never read it.

DORN

You only read what you don't understand.

MEDVEDENKO

What books I have, I read.

DORN

All you read is Buckle and Spencer.[14] You don't know any more than a night watchman. According to you, the heart is made of cartilege and the earth rests on whales.

MEDVEDENKO

The earth is round.

DORN

You don't say that with much conviction.

MEDVEDENKO

(Hurt) When you've got nothing to eat, it's all the same whether the earth is round or rectangular. Don't pick on me, please.

ARKADINA

(Annoyed) Stop it, gentlemen.] *(Reads a few lines to herself)* Well, the rest is uninteresting and inaccurate. *(Closes the book)* My heart's

uneasy. Tell me, what's happened to my son? Why is he so sullen and surly? He spends whole days on the lake, and I hardly ever see him.

MASHA

He's in low spirits. *(To Nina, timidly)* Please, recite something from his play!

NINA

(Shrugging) You want me to? It's so uninteresting.

[*(Reciting)* "People, lions, eagles and partridges, antlered deer, geese, spiders, silent fish inhabiting the waters, starfish and those not visible to the eye—in short, all living things, all living things, all living things have completed their sad round and are extinct . . . For thousands of years already the earth has not borne upon itself a single living being, and this poor moon lights its lamp in vain. The cranes no longer awaken with a cry in the meadows, nor are the june bugs heard in the linden groves."]

MASHA

(Restraining her rapture) [How poetic!] When he himself recites, his eyes glow and his face turns pale. He has a beautiful, mournful voice, and the manners of a poet.

Sorin snores loudly.

DORN

Good night!

ARKADINA

Petrusha!

SORIN

Wha . . . ?

ARKADINA

Are you asleep?

SORIN

Not at all.

Pause.

ARKADINA

You don't take any medications, and that's not good, brother.

SORIN

I'd be glad to, but the doctor here is against it.

DORN

Medications at the age of sixty!

SORIN

Even at sixty you still want to live.

DORN

(Annoyed) Ehh! Well, so, take valerian drops.

ARKADINA

I think it would be good for him to go to a spa somewhere.

DORN

Why not? He could go. Or he could not go.

ARKADINA

Try figuring that out!

DORN

There's nothing to figure out. It's all clear.

Pause.

MEDVEDENKO

Pyotr Nikolaich ought to quit smoking.

[DORN

He ought to have quit long ago. Tobacco and drink are vile.]

SORIN

Nonsense.

DORN

No, it's not nonsense. Drink and tobacco depersonalize a man. After a cigar or a glass of vodka you're no longer Pyotr Nikolaich, you're Pyotr plus somebody else; your "I" gets diffused, and you start treating yourself like a third person—him.

SORIN

(Laughs) It's all very well for you to talk. You've lived your life— but me? I worked in the Justice Department for twenty-eight years, but I haven't lived yet, I've never experienced anything finally, and needless to say I want very much to live. [Your place is filled with embroidered cushions, slippers, and all that, like some sort of museum.] You're sated and indifferent, and so you're inclined to philosophize, but I want to live, and so I drink sherry at dinner and smoke cigars and all that. That's all.

DORN

Life must be taken seriously, and taking medications at the age of sixty, regretting that you had so little pleasure when you were young—forgive me, but that is mere frivolity. It's time to think about the eternal.

MASHA

(Stands up) It must be time for lunch. *(Walks at a lazy, sluggish pace)* My foot's asleep . . . *(Exits)*

DORN

She'll go and down a couple of glasses before lunch.

SORIN

She's not happy about her life, poor thing.

ANTON CHEKHOV

DORN

It's nothing, Your Excellency.

SORIN

You talk like a sated man.

ARKADINA

Ah, what could be more boring than this sweet country boredom! It's hot, still, nobody does anything, everybody philosophizes ... It's good to be with you, friends, it's nice to listen to you, but ... to sit in your hotel room and learn a role—is so much better!

NINA

(Rapturously) Right! How I understand you!

SORIN

Of course, it's better in town. You sit in your study, your valet doesn't admit anybody unannounced, there's the telephone ... cabbies in the street and all that ...

DORN

(Sings softly) "Tell it to her, my flowers ..."

Shamraev enters, followed by Polina Andreevna.

SHAMRAEV

Ah, here they are! Good afternoon! *(Kisses Arkadina's hand, then Nina's)* Very glad to see you in good health. *(To Arkadina)* My wife tells me you intend to go to town with her today. Is it true?

ARKADINA

Yes, we intend to.

SHAMRAEV

Hm ... That's splendid, but how do you plan to get there, my most esteemed lady? We're carting the rye today, all the workmen are busy. And with what horses, may I ask?

ARKADINA

With what horses? How should I know what horses?

SORIN

We do have carriage horses.

SHAMRAEV

(Agitated) Carriage horses? And where will I get collars? Where will I get collars? It's astonishing! It's inconceivable!

[POLINA ANDREEVNA

(To her husband) Stop it, I beg you.

ARKADINA

I don't care about collars or rye . . . I'll go, and that's it.

SHAMRAEV

Irina Nikolaevna, for pity's sake, on what?] My highly esteemed lady! Forgive me, I'm in awe of your talent, I'm ready to give ten years of my life for you, but I cannot give you any horses!

ARKADINA

But what if I have to go? Such a strange business!

SHAMRAEV

My most esteemed lady! You don't know what farming means!

ARKADINA

(Flaring up) The same old story! In that case I'm leaving for Moscow today. Hire me horses in the village, or I'll go to the station on foot!

SHAMRAEV

(Flaring up) In that case I resign my position! Find yourself another steward! *(Exits)*

ARKADINA

It's like this every summer, every summer I get insulted here! I won't set foot here anymore!

She exits left, where the bathhouse is presumed to be; a minute later she is seen going to the house; after her walks Trigorin with fishing rods and a bucket.

SORIN

(Flaring up) That is impudence! That is the devil knows what! I'm sick of it finally. Have all the horses brought here at once!

NINA

(To Polina Andreevna) To refuse Irina Nikolaevna, a famous actress! Isn't her every wish, or even caprice, more important than your farming? It's simply incredible!

POLINA ANDREEVNA

(In despair) What can I do? Put yourself in my place: what can I do?

[SORIN

He's leaving, abandoning the farm at the hottest time, and all that. I won't let him! I'll make him stay!

DORN

Pyotr Nikolaich, show at least a pennyworth of character!]

SORIN

(To Nina) Let's go to my sister . . . We'll all beg her not to leave. Right? *(Looking in the direction in which Shamraev went)* An insufferable man! A despot!

NINA

(Keeping him from standing up) Sit, sit . . . We'll take you there . . . *(She and Medvedenko roll the chair)* Oh, it's so awful! . . .

SORIN

Yes, yes, it's awful . . . But he won't leave, I'll have a talk with him right now.

They exit; only Dorn and Polina Andreevna remain.

DORN

People are boring. In fact, your husband ought simply to be thrown out on his ear, but it will all end with that old woman Pyotr Nikolaich and his sister apologizing to him. You'll see!

POLINA ANDREEVNA

He sent the carriage horses to the fields, too. And there are misunderstandings like that every day. If only you knew how it upsets me! I get ill—see, I'm trembling. I can't bear his coarseness. *(Pleadingly)* Evgeny, my dearest, my darling, take me away . . . Our time is running out, we're not young anymore, at the end of our lives we can at least stop hiding and lying . . .

Pause.

DORN

I'm fifty-five years old, it's too late to change my life.

POLINA ANDREEVNA

I know, you refuse me because there are women besides me who are close to you. You can't take them all away. I understand. Forgive me, I'm wearying you.

Nina appears by the house; she picks flowers.

DORN

No, it's nothing.

POLINA ANDREEVNA

I suffer from jealousy. Of course, you're a doctor, you can't avoid women. I understand that . . .

DORN

(To Nina, who is approaching) How is it there?

NINA

Irina Nikolaevna is crying, and Pyotr Nikolaich is having asthma.

DORN

(Gets up) I'll go and give them both valerian drops . . .

NINA

(Offering him flowers) Here, please!

DORN

Merci bien. (He goes toward the house)

POLINA ANDREEVNA

(Going with him) What sweet flowers! *(Near the house, in a hollow voice)* Give me those flowers! Give me those flowers!

He hands her the flowers; she tears them to pieces and throws them away. They go into the house.

NINA

(Alone) How strange to see a well-known actress cry, and for such a silly reason! And isn't it strange that a famous writer, the darling of the public, written about in all the newspapers, his portrait for sale, translated into foreign languages, spends the whole day fishing and rejoices at catching two chubs? I thought well-known people were proud, inaccessible, that they scorned the crowd. And by their fame, the brilliance of their name, they took a sort of revenge on the crowd, for placing noble birth and wealth highest of all. But there they are crying, catching fish, playing cards, laughing and getting angry, like everybody else . . . [They're modest. Yesterday I asked him for his autograph, and as a joke he wrote some bad verses, deliberately bad, to make everybody laugh . . .]

TREPLYOV

(Enters, hatless, with a gun and a dead seagull) You're here alone?

NINA

Yes.

Treplyov lays the seagull at her feet.

What does this mean?

TREPLYOV

I was vile enough to kill this seagull today. I lay it at your feet.

NINA

What's the matter with you? *(Picks up the seagull and looks at it)*

TREPLYOV

(After a pause) Soon I'll kill myself the same way.

NINA

I don't recognize you.

TREPLYOV

Yes, after I stopped recognizing you. You've changed towards me, your look is cold, my presence cramps you.

NINA

You've grown irritable lately, you express yourself incomprehensibly, in symbols of some kind. And this seagull is also apparently a symbol, but, forgive me, I don't understand . . . *(Puts the seagull on the bench)* I'm too simple to understand you.

TREPLYOV

It began that evening when my play failed so stupidly. Women don't forgive failure. I burned it all, all of it to the last scrap. If only you knew how unhappy I am! Your coldness is frightening, incredible, like waking up and seeing that the lake, there, has suddenly dried up or seeped into the ground. You just said you're too simple to understand me. Oh, what's there to understand?! You didn't like the play, you despise my inspiration, you consider me a mediocrity, a nonentity, one of many . . . *(Stamps his foot)* How well I understand that, how I understand! It's like there's a nail in my brain, may it be cursed along with my vanity, which sucks my blood, sucks it like a snake . . . *(Seeing Trigorin, who walks reading a book)* Here comes a true talent; he strides along like Hamlet, and with a book as well. *(Teasing)* "Words, words, words . . ." This sun hasn't even come up to you yet, and you're already smiling, your glance melts in its rays. I won't bother you. *(Exits quickly)*

TRIGORIN

(Writes in his notebook) Takes snuff and drinks vodka . . . Always wears black. The teacher loves her . . .

NINA

Good morning, Boris Alexeich!

TRIGORIN

Good morning. Owing to unforeseen circumstances, it seems we're leaving today. It's unlikely we'll see each other again. And that's a pity. I don't often get to meet young girls, young and interesting; I've already forgotten and cannot picture clearly to myself how it feels to be eighteen or nineteen, and therefore in my novellas and stories young girls usually come out false. I'd like to be in your place for just an hour, to find out how you think and generally what sort of little thing you are.

NINA

And I'd like to be in your place.

TRIGORIN

What for?

NINA

To find out how a famous, talented writer feels. How does fame feel? What do you feel like, being famous?

TRIGORIN

What? Whatever. I've never thought about it. *(After reflecting)* It's one of two things: either you're exaggerating my fame, or there's no feeling to it at all.

NINA

And when you read about yourself in the newspapers?

TRIGORIN

When they praise me, it feels good, and when they abuse me, I feel out of sorts for two days afterwards.

NINA

A wondrous world! If only you knew how I envy you! Destinies are different. Some people barely drag out their dull, inconspicuous existence, they're all the same, they're all unhappy; others, like you, for instance—you're one in a million—are granted an interesting life, bright, full of meaning . . . You're happy . . .

TRIGORIN

Me? *(Shrugs)* Hm . . . You talk about fame, about happiness, about some sort of bright, interesting life, but for me all these nice words, forgive me, are so much candied fruit, which I never eat. You're very young and very kind.

NINA

Your life is beautiful!

TRIGORIN

What's so especially good about it? *(Looks at his watch)* I must go now and write. Sorry, I have no time . . . *(Laughs)* You've touched my pet sore spot, as they say, and I'm beginning to get agitated and a little bit angry. Very well, let's talk. We'll talk about my beautiful, bright life . . . Well, miss, where shall we begin? *(Reflects a little)* There exist certain obsessions, when a person thinks day and night, for instance, about nothing but the moon. Well, I have my own such moon. Day and night I'm beset by one nagging thought: I must write, I must write, I must . . . I've barely finished one story, when for some reason I must write another, then a third, and after the third a fourth . . . I write nonstop, like with post-horses, and can't do otherwise. What's so beautiful and bright in that, I ask you? Oh, what a brutish life! Here I am with you, I'm agitated, and meanwhile every moment I remember that an unfinished story is waiting for me. Say I see a cloud that looks like a grand piano. I think: I must mention somewhere in a story that a cloud drifted over that looked like a grand piano. There's a smell of heliotrope. I quickly make a mental note of it: sickly sweet smell, widow color, mention in a description of a summer evening. I catch us both up at every phrase, every word, and hasten to quickly lock away all these phrases and words in my literary storeroom: maybe they'll be of use! When I finish work, I run to the theater or go fishing; here's my chance to rest, to forget myself—but, no, a heavy iron ball is already rolling around in my head—a new subject, and I'm already drawn to my desk, and again have to hurriedly start writing and writing. And it's always, always like that, and I get no rest from myself, and I feel that I'm eating up my own life, that for the sake of the honey I give to somebody out there, I gather pollen from my best flowers, tear up the flowers themselves and trample on their roots. Am I not crazy? Do my friends and acquaintances treat me like a sane man? "What are you writing these days? What are you going to bestow on us?" The same thing, the same thing, and it seems to me that this attention from acquaintances, the praise, the admiration—are all a deception, that I'm being deceived like a sick man, and I'm sometimes afraid they're about to sneak up on me from behind, seize me, and take me to the madhouse like Gogol's Poprishchin.[15] And in those years, in my best, young years, when I was just beginning, my writing was one unbroken torment. A minor writer, especially if he has no luck, seems clumsy to himself, awkward, superfluous, his nerves are strained, overwrought; he wanders helplessly among people connected with literature and art, unacknowledged, unnoticed by anyone, afraid to look anyone straight and boldly in the eye, like a passionate gambler who has no money. I had never seen my reader, but in my imagination I pictured him for some reason as unfriendly, mistrustful. I was afraid of the public, it frightened me, and when I had to put on a new play, it seemed to me each time that the dark-haired people were hostile and the fair-haired coldly indifferent. Oh, it was terrible! What torture!

NINA

Excuse me, but doesn't inspiration and the process of creation itself give you lofty, happy moments?

TRIGORIN

Yes. It's pleasant while I'm writing. And it's pleasant reading proofs, but . . . the moment it comes out in print, I can't stand it, I see it's all wrong, a mistake, that I should never have written it in the first place, and I'm annoyed, there's a rotten feeling in my soul . . . *(Laughs)* And the public reads it: "Yes, nice, talented . . . Nice, but a far cry from Tolstoy," or: "An excellent thing, but Turgenev's *Fathers and Sons* is better." And so till my coffin closes it will all only be nice and talented, nice and talented—nothing more. And when I die, my acquaintances, passing by my grave, will say: "Here lies Trigorin. He was a good writer, but not as good as Turgenev."

NINA

Forgive me, but I can't accept that. You're simply spoiled by success.

TRIGORIN

What success? I've never liked myself. I don't like myself as a writer. Worst of all, I get into a sort of daze and often don't understand what I write . . . I love this water here, the trees, the sky. I feel nature, it arouses a passion in me, an overwhelming desire to write. But I'm not just a landscape painter, I'm also a citizen. I love my country, my people, I feel if I'm a writer, it's my duty to speak about the people, about their sufferings, their future, to speak about science, about human rights, etcetera, etcetera, and I do speak about all that, I push myself, people come at me from all sides, get angry, I rush this way and that, like a fox hunted down by dogs, I see life and science keep going forward, and I keep lagging behind, like a peasant late for the train, and in the end I feel I can only paint landscapes, and in all the rest I'm false, false to the marrow of my bones.

NINA

You work too much, and you have neither the time nor the desire to be aware of your own importance. You may be dissatisfied with yourself, but for others you're great and wonderful! If I were such a writer, I'd give my whole life to the crowd, aware all the while that their happiness lies only in rising to my heights, and they would drive me around in a chariot.

TRIGORIN

Oh, yes, in a chariot . . . What am I—Agamemnon?

They both smile.

NINA

For the happiness of being a writer or an actress, I'd give up the love of my family, endure poverty, disappointment. I'd live in an attic and eat nothing but black bread. I'd suffer from being dissatisfied with myself, from the awareness of my imperfections, but in return I would demand fame . . . real, resounding fame . . . *(Covers her face with her hands)* My head's spinning . . . Oof! . . .

Arkadina's voice from the house: "Boris Alexeich!"

TRIGORIN

They're calling me . . . Must be time to pack. And I don't feel like leaving. *(Turns to look at the lake)* Just look at this blessedness! . . . How good!

NINA

See that house and garden on the other side?

TRIGORIN

Yes.

NINA

That's my late mother's estate. I was born there. I've spent my whole life by this lake and know every little island in it.

TRIGORIN

It's so good here! *(Seeing the seagull)* What's that?

NINA

A seagull. Konstantin Gavrilych killed it.

TRIGORIN

A beautiful bird. I really don't feel like leaving. Why don't you persuade Irina Nikolaevna to stay? *(Writes in his notebook)*

NINA

What are you writing?

TRIGORIN

Just some notes . . . A subject came to me . . . *(Putting away the notebook)* A subject for a short story: all her life a young girl, like you, has lived on the shore of a lake. She loves the lake, like a seagull, and she's happy and free like a seagull. But a man happens along, sees her, and, having nothing better to do, destroys her, like this seagull here.

Pause. Arkadina appears in the window.

ARKADINA

Boris Alexeich, where are you?

TRIGORIN

Coming! *(Goes, turns to look at Nina; at the window, to Arkadina)*
What is it?

ARKADINA

We're staying.

Trigorin goes into the house.

NINA

(After thinking a moment) A dream!

Curtain.

ACT THREE

The dining room in Sorin's house. Doors to the right and left. A sideboard. A medicine chest. A table in the middle of the room. A suitcase and cardboard boxes—signs of preparations for departure. Trigorin is having lunch. Masha stands by the table.

MASHA

I'm telling you all this as a writer. You can make use of it. I tell you honestly: if he had wounded himself seriously, I wouldn't have survived for a minute. But still I'm brave. I just up and decided: I'll tear this love out of my heart, tear it out by the root.

TRIGORIN

How so?

MASHA

I'm getting married. To Medvedenko.

TRIGORIN

You mean the schoolteacher?

MASHA

Yes.

TRIGORIN

I don't see the need.

MASHA

To love hopelessly, to spend whole years waiting for something . . . But once I'm married, there'll be no more question of love; new concerns will stifle all the old things. And anyhow, you know, it's a change. Have another?

TRIGORIN

Won't it be too much?

MASHA

There! *(Pours two glasses)* Don't look at me like that. Women drink more often than you'd think. The minority drink openly, like me, and the majority do it in secret. Yes. Always vodka or cognac. *(Clinks glasses with him)* Here's to you! You're a simple man, it's a pity you're leaving us.

They drink.

TRIGORIN

Personally, I don't want to go.

MASHA

You could ask her to stay.

TRIGORIN

No, she won't stay now. Her son is behaving quite tactlessly. First he tries to shoot himself, and now they say he's going to challenge me to a duel. And for what? He sulks, snorts, preaches new forms . . . But there's room enough for everybody, the new and the old— why start shoving?

MASHA

Well, there's jealousy, too. However, that's none of my business.

Pause. Yakov crosses from left to right with a suitcase; Nina enters and stops by the window.

My teacher is none too bright, but he's a good man and a poor one, and he loves me very much. I feel sorry for him. And for his old mother. Well, sir, allow me to wish you all the best. Think kindly of me. *(Gives him a firm handshake)* I'm very grateful to you for your kind disposition. Do send me your books, and be sure to sign them. Only don't write, "To the most esteemed . . ." but just, "For Marya, last name unknown, who has no idea why she lives in this world." Good-bye! *(Exits)*

NINA

(Holding out a closed fist to Trigorin) Odd or even?

TRIGORIN

Even.

NINA

(With a sigh) No. There's only one pea in my hand. I left it to chance: do I go and become an actress or not? If only someone would advise me.

TRIGORIN

It's impossible to give advice about that.

Pause.

NINA

We're parting and . . . we'll probably never see each other again. I ask you to accept this small medallion from me as a keepsake. I had your initials engraved on it . . . and on this side the title of your book—*Days and Nights.*

TRIGORIN

How graceful! *(Kisses the medallion)* A charming gift!

NINA

Think of me once in a while.

TRIGORIN

I will. I'll think of you the way you were on that clear day—remember?—a week ago, when you were wearing a light-colored dress . . . We talked . . . there was also a white seagull lying on the bench.

NINA

(Pensively) Yes, a seagull . . .

Pause.

We can't talk anymore, somebody's coming . . . Grant me two minutes before you leave, I beg you . . .

She exits left. At the same time from the right enter Arkadina and Sorin, in a tailcoat with a decoration, followed by Yakov, preoccupied with the packing.

ARKADINA

Why don't you stay home, old man. Should you with your rheumatism be driving around visiting people? *(To Trigorin)* Who just left? Nina?

TRIGORIN

Yes.

ARKADINA

Pardon, we disturbed you . . . *(Sits down)* I think everything's packed. I'm exhausted.

TRIGORIN

(Reads from the medallion) Days and Nights, page 121, lines 11 and 12.

YAKOV

(Clearing the table) Do you want me to pack the fishing rods as well?

TRIGORIN

Yes, I'll be needing them. And give the books away to somebody.

YAKOV

Yes, sir.

TRIGORIN

(To himself) Page 121, lines 11 and 12. What's in those lines? *(To Arkadina)* Do you have my books here in the house?

ARKADINA

In my brother's study, in the corner bookcase.

TRIGORIN

Page 121 . . . *(Exits)*

ARKADINA

Really, Petrusha, you'd better stay home . . .

SORIN

You're leaving. It will be hard for me here without you.

ARKADINA

And what is there in town?

SORIN

Nothing special, but still . . . *(Laughs)* There'll be the laying of the cornerstone for the local council building and all that . . . I'd like to rouse myself from this slug's life for an hour or two, I've been stagnating here too long, like an old pipe. I ordered them to bring the horses by one o'clock. We'll set out at the same time.

ARKADINA

(After a pause) Live here now, don't get bored, don't catch cold. Keep an eye on my son. Take care of him. Guide him.

Pause.

I'll go away, and never know why Konstantin tried to shoot himself. It seems to me the main thing was jealousy, and the sooner I take Trigorin away from here, the better.

SORIN

What can I tell you? There were also other things. Needless to say, a young man, intelligent, living in the country, in the backwoods, with no money, no position, no future. Nothing to occupy him. He's ashamed and afraid of his idleness. I'm extremely fond of him, and he's attached to me, but still in the end it seems to him that he's superfluous here, a parasite, a sponger. Needless to say, self-esteem . . .

ARKADINA

What a trial he is to me! *(Reflecting)* Maybe he should get himself a job or something . . .

SORIN

(Whistles, then hesitantly) It seems to me it would be best if you . . . gave him a little money. First, he needs to dress like a human being and all that. Look, he's been wearing the same wretched frock coat for three years, he goes around without an overcoat . . . *(Laughs)* And it wouldn't hurt for the boy to have some fun . . . To go abroad or something . . . It's not so expensive.

ARKADINA

Still . . . Maybe for a suit of clothes, but to go abroad . . . No, right now not even for a suit of clothes. *(Resolutely)* I have no money!

Sorin laughs.

No!

SORIN
(Whistles) Right, ma'am. Forgive me, dear, don't be angry. I believe you . . . You're a magnanimous, noble woman.

ARKADINA
(Through tears) I have no money!

SORIN
If I had money, needless to say, I'd give it to him, but I have nothing, not even five kopecks. *(Laughs)* The steward takes my whole pension and spends it on farming, cattle breeding, beekeeping, and the money's wasted. The bees drop dead, the cows drop dead, the horses are never there when you need them . . .

ARKADINA
Yes, I do have money, but I'm an actress; the clothes alone ruin me.

SORIN
You're kind, sweet . . . I respect you . . . Yes . . . But something's wrong with me again . . . *(Staggers)* My head's spinning . . . *(Holds on to the table)* I feel faint and all that.

ARKADINA
(Frightened) Petrusha! *(Tries to support him)* Petrusha, dearest . . . *(Shouts)* Help me! Help! . . .

Enter Treplyov, with a bandaged head, and Medvedenko.

He's fainting!

SORIN
It's nothing, nothing . . . *(Smiles and drinks water)* It's already over . . . and all that . . .

TREPLYOV

(To his mother) Don't be afraid, mama, it's not dangerous. It often happens to uncle now. *(To his uncle)* You should lie down, uncle.

SORIN

For a little, yes . . . But I'll go to town anyway . . . I'll lie down and then go . . . needless to say . . . *(Starts to leave, leaning on his cane)*

MEDVEDENKO

(Leading him by the arm) There's this riddle: on four in the morning, on two at noon, on three in the evening . . .[16]

SORIN

(Laughs) Precisely. And on its back at night. Thank you, I can go by myself . . .

MEDVEDENKO

So, now you're standing on ceremony! . . . *(He and Sorin exit)*

ARKADINA

How he frightened me!

TREPLYOV

It's not healthy for him to live in the country. He languishes. If you suddenly opened your purse, mama, and lent him fifteen hundred or two thousand, he could live in town for a whole year.

ARKADINA

I have no money. I'm an actress, not a banker.

Pause.

TREPLYOV

Mama, change my bandage. You do it so well.

ARKADINA

(Takes iodine and a box of bandaging from the medicine chest) The doctor's late.

TREPLYOV

He promised to come at ten, and it's already noon.

ARKADINA

Sit down. *(Takes his bandage off)* It's like a turban. Yesterday in the kitchen a visitor asked what nationality you were. It's nearly healed. Barely a trace left. *(Kisses him on the head)* And you won't go click-click again when I'm not here?

TREPLYOV

No, mama. That was a moment of wild desperation, when I lost control of myself. It won't happen again. *(Kisses her hand)* You have golden hands. I remember, very long ago, when you were still working in the state theaters—I was a little boy then—there was a fight in our courtyard, and a washerwoman, a tenant, was badly beaten. Remember? They picked her up unconscious . . . you kept visiting her, bringing her medicines, washing her children in a tub. Don't you remember?

ARKADINA

No. *(Applies a new bandage)*

TREPLYOV

Two ballet dancers lived in the same house with us . . . They'd come and have coffee with you . . .

ARKADINA

That I remember.

TREPLYOV

They were very pious.

Pause.

Just recently, in these past few days, I've loved you as tenderly and wholeheartedly as when I was a child. I have no one left now but you. Only why, why has this man come between us?

ARKADINA

You don't understand him, Konstantin. He is the noblest person . . .

TREPLYOV

Yet when he was told I was going to challenge him to a duel, his nobility didn't keep him from turning coward. He's leaving. Shamefully running away!

ARKADINA

What nonsense! I myself am taking him away. You, of course, cannot like our intimacy, but you're intelligent and sophisticated, and I have the right to demand that you respect my freedom.

TREPLYOV

I respect your freedom. But you, too, must allow me to be free, and to have my own opinion of this man. The noblest person! Here you and I are almost quarreling because of him, and he's somewhere in the drawing room now, or in the garden, laughing at us . . . improving Nina, trying to finally convince her that he's a genius.

ARKADINA

You delight in saying unpleasant things to me. I respect this man and beg you not to speak ill of him in my presence.

TREPLYOV

Well, I don't respect him. You want me to consider him a genius, too, but—sorry—I'm no good at lying, his writing repulses me.

ARKADINA

That's jealousy. For people who have no talent but do have pretensions, there's nothing left but to denounce real talent. A nice consolation!

TREPLYOV

(Ironically) Real talent! *(Angrily)* I'm more talented than all of you, if it comes down to that! *(Tears bandage off his head)* You slaves to the rut have seized first place in art and think that only what you yourselves do is legitimate and genuine, and all the rest you oppress and stifle! I don't acknowledge you! Neither you nor him!

ARKADINA

Decadent!

TREPLYOV

Go off to your precious theater and perform your pathetic, giftless plays!

ARKADINA

I have never acted in such plays. Leave me alone! You can't even write a pitiful little farce! Kiev tradesman! Sponger!

TREPLYOV

Skinflint!

ARKADINA

Ragpicker!

Treplyov sits down and cries softly.

Nonentity! *(Paces nervously)* Don't cry. You shouldn't cry . . . *(Cries)* You mustn't . . . *(Kisses him on the forehead, cheeks, head)* My dear child, forgive me . . . Forgive your sinful mother. Forgive an unhappy woman!

TREPLYOV

(Embraces her) If only you knew! I've lost everything. She doesn't love me, I can't write anymore . . . My hopes are all gone . . .

ARKADINA

Don't despair . . . Everything will turn out well. I'm taking him away now, and she'll love you again. *(Wipes his tears)* Enough. We've made peace.

TREPLYOV

(Kissing her hands) Yes, mama.

ARKADINA

(Tenderly) Make peace with him, too. There's no need for a duel . . . No need, is there?

TREPLYOV

All right . . . Only let me not meet him, mama. It's hard for me . . . beyond my strength . . .

Enter Trigorin.

There . . . I'm leaving . . . *(Quickly puts the medical things back in the chest)* The doctor will do the bandaging . . .

TRIGORIN

(Searching in the book) Page 121 . . . lines 11 and 12 . . . Here . . . *(Reads)* "If you ever need my life, come and take it."

Treplyov picks up the bandage from the floor and exits.

ARKADINA

(Looking at her watch) They'll bring the horses soon.

TRIGORIN

(To himself) If you ever need my life, come and take it.

ARKADINA

You're all packed, I hope?

TRIGORIN

(Impatiently) Yes, yes . . . *(Pondering)* Why is it that I hear sorrow in this appeal of a pure soul and my heart is so painfully wrung? . . . If you ever need my life, come and take it. *(To Arkadina)* Let's stay one more day!

Arkadina shakes her head negatively.

Let's stay!

ARKADINA

My dear, I know what keeps you here. But control yourself. You're a little drunk—sober up.

TRIGORIN

You be sober, too, be sensible, reasonable, I beg you, look at it all as a true friend . . . *(Presses her hand)* You're capable of sacrifice . . . Be my friend, release me . . .

ARKADINA

(In great agitation) Are you so infatuated?

TRIGORIN

I'm drawn to her! Maybe it's precisely what I need.

ARKADINA

The love of a provincial girl? Oh, how little you know yourself!

TRIGORIN

Sometimes people walk in their sleep, so here I am talking to you, and it's as if I'm asleep and seeing her in my dreams . . . I'm overcome by sweet, wondrous dreams . . . Release me . . .

ARKADINA

(Trembling) No, no . . . I'm an ordinary woman, you can't talk to me like that . . . Don't torment me, Boris . . . I'm frightened . . .

TRIGORIN

You can be extraordinary, if you wish. Love—youthful, charming, poetic, that carries you off to the world of dreams—that alone can give happiness on earth! I've never experienced such love before ... When I was young, I had no time, I haunted the doorways of publishers, struggled with poverty ... Now here it is, this love, it has finally come, it's beckoning to me ... What's the sense of running away from it?

ARKADINA

(Angrily) You're out of your mind!

TRIGORIN

So I am.

ARKADINA

You've all conspired to torment me today! *(Cries)*

TRIGORIN

(Clutching his head) She doesn't understand! Doesn't want to understand!

ARKADINA

Am I so old and ugly that you can talk to me about other women without feeling embarrassed? *(Embraces him and kisses him)* Oh, you've gone mad! My wonderful, marvelous one ... You're the last page of my life! *(Goes on her knees)* My joy, my pride, my bliss ... *(Embraces his knees)* If you abandon me even for one hour, I won't survive, I'll go out of my mind, my amazing, magnificent one, my lord and master ...

TRIGORIN

Somebody may come in. *(Helps her to her feet)*

ARKADINA

Let them, I'm not ashamed of my love for you. *(Kisses his hands)* My treasure, my desperate one, you want to run wild, but I don't want it, I won't let you . . . *(Laughs)* You're mine . . . mine . . . This forehead is mine, and these eyes are mine, and this beautiful silken hair is also mine . . . You're all mine. You're so talented, intelligent, the best of all today's writers, you're Russia's only hope . . . You have so much sincerity, simplicity, freshness, healthy humor . . . With one stroke you can convey the main thing that characterizes a person or a landscape, your people are as if alive. Oh, it's impossible to read you without rapture! You think this is all just incense? That I'm flattering you? Well, look me in the eye . . . look . . . Do I look like a liar? You can see I'm the only one who knows how to appreciate you; the only one who tells you the truth, my dear, wonderful one . . . You'll come? Yes? You won't abandon me? . . .

TRIGORIN

I have no will of my own . . . I've never had a will of my own . . . Limp, lax, always submissive—can a woman possibly like that? Take me, carry me off, only don't let me go one step away from you . . .

ARKADINA

{*(To herself)* Now he's mine.} *(Casually, as if nothing had happened)* However, you may stay, if you wish. I'll go by myself, and you can come later, in a week. Actually, why should you hurry?

TRIGORIN

No, we'll go together.

ARKADINA

As you wish. If it's together, it's together.

Pause. Trigorin writes in his notebook.

What's this now?

TRIGORIN

I heard a nice expression this morning: "The maidens' pine grove . . ." It may come in handy. *(Stretches)* So we're going? Again coaches, stations, buffets, cutlets, small talk . . .

Enter Shamraev.

SHAMRAEV

I have the honor of announcing regretfully that the horses are ready. It's time, my most esteemed lady, to go to the station; the train comes at 2:05. And kindly do not forget, Irina Nikolaevna, to make inquiries as to the present whereabouts of the actor Suzdaltsev. Is he alive? Is he in good health? We used to drink together once upon a time . . . He performed inimitably in *The Great Mail Robbery* . . . [17] He worked in Elisavetgrad then, as I recall, with the tragedian Izmailov—also a remarkable person . . . Don't rush, my most esteemed lady, we still have five minutes. They once played accomplices in a melodrama, and when they were suddenly caught, the line was supposed to be: "We fell into a trap," but Izmailov said: "We tell into a frap . . ." *(Laughs loudly)* Into a frap! . . .

While he talks, Yakov busies himself with the luggage, the maid brings Arkadina a hat, a cloak, an umbrella, gloves; they all help Arkadina to dress. The cook peeks through the door left, and a little later enters hesitantly. Enter Polina Andreevna, then Sorin and Medvedenko.

POLINA ANDREEVNA

(With a little basket) Here are some plums for you for the road. Very sweet ones. Maybe you'll want a treat . . .

ARKADINA

You're very kind, Polina Andreevna.

POLINA ANDREEVNA

Good-bye, my dear! If anything wasn't right, forgive me. *(Cries)*

ARKADINA

(Embraces her) Everything was fine, everything was fine. Just don't cry.

POLINA ANDREEVNA

Our time is running out!

ARKADINA

Can't be helped!

SORIN

(Wearing a greatcoat, a hat, carrying a stick, enters from the door left; walks across the room) It's time, sister, we may be late and all that. I'm going to get in. *(Exits)*

MEDVEDENKO

And I'll go to the station on foot . . . to see you off. I'll walk fast . . . *(Exits)*

ARKADINA

Good-bye, my dears . . . If we're alive and well, we'll see each other again next summer . . .

Yakov, the maid and the cook kiss her hand.

Don't forget me. *(Gives the cook a ruble)* Here's a ruble for the three of you.

COOK

We humbly thank you, ma'am. Have a good trip. We're much pleased!

YAKOV

God give you good luck!

SHAMRAEV

We'd be so happy for a little letter from you! Good-bye, Boris Alexeich! . . .

ARKADINA
Where's Konstantin? Tell him I'm leaving. We must say good-bye. Well, think kindly of us. *(To Yakov)* I've given the cook a ruble. For the three of you.

All exit right. The stage is empty. From backstage come the noises of people saying good-bye. The maid comes back onstage to take the basket of plums from the table. Exits again.

TRIGORIN
(Coming back) Forgot my cane. I think it's there on the terrace. *(Goes to the door left and runs into Nina)* It's you? We're leaving . . .

NINA
I had a feeling we'd see each other again. *(Excitedly)* Boris Alexeich, I've decided once and for all, the die is cast, I'm going on the stage. Tomorrow I'll no longer be here, I'm leaving my father, I'm abandoning everything and beginning a new life . . . I'm leaving, like you . . . for Moscow. We'll see each other there.

TRIGORIN
(Looking around) Stay at the Slavyansky Bazar hotel . . . Let me know at once . . . Molchanovka Street, Grokholsky's house . . . I must hurry . . .

Pause.

NINA
One more moment . . .

TRIGORIN
(In a low voice) You're so beautiful . . . Oh, what happiness to think we'll see each other soon!

She leans on his chest.

Again I'll see these wonderful eyes, the inexpressibly beautiful, tender smile . . . these gentle features, the look of angelic purity . . . My dear . . .

A prolonged kiss.

Curtain.

Between Acts Three and Four two years pass.

ACT FOUR

One of the drawing rooms in Sorin's house, which Treplyov has turned into a study. Doors to the right and left leading to inner rooms. Straight ahead a glass door to the terrace. Besides the usual drawing room furniture, there is a desk in the corner right, a Turkish divan by the door left, a bookcase, books on windowsills and chairs.

Evening. One lamp burns under a shade. Semidarkness. The sound of rustling trees and of wind howling in the chimneys. The watchman raps on his board.

Medvedenko and Masha enter.

MASHA

(Calls out) Konstantin Gavrilych! Konstantin Gavrilych! *(Looking around)* Nobody's here. The old man keeps asking all the time, where's Kostya, where's Kostya . . . He can't live without him . . .

MEDVEDENKO

He's afraid to be alone. *(Listening)* What awful weather! It's already the second day.

MASHA

(Turning up the light in the lamp) There are waves on the lake. Enormous.

MEDVEDENKO

It's dark in the garden. They should be told to knock down that theater. It stands there in the garden, bare, ugly as a skeleton, and the curtain flaps in the wind. When I passed by last evening, it seemed as if somebody was crying in it.

MASHA

Well, so . . .

Pause.

MEDVEDENKO

Let's go home, Masha!

MASHA

(Shakes her head negatively) I'll spend the night here.

MEDVEDENKO

(Pleading) Masha, let's go! Our baby must be hungry.

MASHA

Nonsense. Matryona will feed him.

Pause.

MEDVEDENKO

It's a pity. Three nights now without his mother.

MASHA

What a bore you've become. Before at least you'd philosophize, but now it's baby, home, baby, home—that's all I ever hear from you.

MEDVEDENKO

Let's go, Masha!

MASHA

Go yourself.

MEDVEDENKO

Your father won't give me a horse.

MASHA

Yes, he will. Ask him, and he'll give you one.

MEDVEDENKO

I guess I can ask. So you'll come tomorrow?

MASHA

(Taking snuff) All right, tomorrow. Pest . . .

Enter Treplyov and Polina Andreevna; Treplyov brings pillows and a blanket, and Polina Andreevna bedsheets; they set them down on the Turkish divan, then Treplyov goes to his desk and sits down.

What's that for, mama?

POLINA ANDREEVNA

Pyotr Nikolaich asked me to make a bed for him in Kostya's study.

MASHA

Here, let me . . . *(Starts making the bed)*

POLINA ANDREEVNA

(With a sigh) An old man is a child twice over . . . *(Goes to desk and, leaning her elbows on it, looks into a manuscript)*

Pause.

MEDVEDENKO

I'll be going, then. Good-bye, Masha. *(Kisses his wife's hand)* Good-bye, mother. *(Wants to kiss his mother-in-law's hand)*

POLINA ANDREEVNA

(Annoyed) Enough! Off you go!

MEDVEDENKO

Good-bye, Konstantin Gavrilych.

Treplyov silently gives him his hand; Medvedenko exits.

POLINA ANDREEVNA

(Looking into manuscript) Nobody would have thought that a real writer would come of you, Kostya. And now, thank God, the magazines have even started sending you money. *(Strokes his hair)* And you've grown handsome . . . Dear, good Kostya, be nicer to my Mashenka! . . .

MASHA

(Making the bed) Leave him alone, mama.

POLINA ANDREEVNA

(To Treplyov) She's a nice, sweet girl.

Pause.

A woman needs nothing, Kostya, only a tender look. I know from myself.

Treplyov gets up from his desk and silently exits.

MASHA

Now you've made him angry. You just had to pester him!

POLINA ANDREEVNA

I feel sorry for you, Mashenka.

MASHA

As if I need that!

POLINA ANDREEVNA

My heart aches for you. I see it all, I understand it all.

MASHA

It's all foolishness. Hopeless love—that's only for novels. Nonsense. The only thing is not to give in to it, not to keep waiting, waiting for something, for the sky to clear . . . If love gets into your heart, get it out. They've promised to transfer my husband to another district. Once we move there—I'll forget everything . . . I'll tear it out of my heart by the root.

Two rooms away someone starts playing a melancholy waltz.

POLINA ANDREEVNA

Kostya's playing. That means he's feeling sad.

MASHA

(Soundlessly makes two or three turns of the waltz) The main thing, mama, is not to have it in front of my eyes. If only my Semyon gets transferred, believe me, I'll forget about it in a month. It's all nonsense.

The door left opens, Dorn and Medvedenko roll in Sorin in the wheelchair.

MEDVEDENKO

I've got six at home now. And flour is over two kopecks a pound.

DORN

That'll keep you juggling.

MEDVEDENKO

It's fine for you to laugh. You've got money coming out of your ears.

DORN

Money? Out of thirty years of practice, my friend, of stressful practice, when I didn't belong to myself day or night, I managed to save only two thousand, and I just recently ran through it all abroad. I've got nothing.

MASHA

(To her husband) You haven't left yet?

MEDVEDENKO

(Guiltily) How can I? He won't give me a horse!

MASHA

(Bitterly, in a low voice) I can't stand the sight of you!

The wheelchair stops on the left side of the room; Polina Andreevna, Masha and Dorn sit down by it; Medvedenko, saddened, retreats to the other side.

DORN

Look at all the changes! The drawing room's become a study.

MASHA

Konstantin Gavrilych is more comfortable working here. Whenever he likes, he can go out to the garden and think there.

The watchman raps.

SORIN

Where's my sister?

DORN

She went to the station to meet Trigorin. She'll be back any minute.

SORIN

If you found it necessary to send for my sister, that means I'm dangerously ill. *(After a pause)* It's funny! I'm dangerously ill, yet I'm not given any medications.

DORN

What would you like? Valerian drops? Soda? Quinine?

SORIN

So the philosophizing begins. Oh, what punishment! *(Nodding toward the divan)* Was that made up for me?

POLINA ANDREEVNA

Yes, for you, Pyotr Nikolaich.

SORIN

I thank you.

DORN

(Singing softly) "The moon sails through the night sky . . ."[18]

SORIN

I'd like to give Kostya a subject for a story. It should be entitled: "The Man Who Wanted." *"L'homme qui a voulu."* When I was young, I wanted to become a writer—and I didn't become one; I wanted to speak beautifully—and I spoke disgustingly . . . *(Imitates himself)* "And all, and all that, sort of, sort of not . . ." and my closing statements would drag on and on, I'd even break into a sweat; I wanted to get married—and I didn't get married; I always wanted to live in town—and here I'm ending my life in the country and all that.

DORN

You wanted to become an actual state councillor—and you became one.

SORIN

(Laughs) I didn't go after it. It came by itself.

DORN

To express dissatisfaction with life at the age of sixty-two, you'll admit—is not very generous.

SORIN

What a pighead. Try to understand, I want to live!

DORN

That's mere frivolity. By the laws of nature every life must have an end.

SORIN

You reason like a sated man. You're sated and therefore indifferent to life, it's all the same to you. But you, too, will be afraid to die.

DORN

The fear of death is an animal fear . . . It must be suppressed. Only believers in eternal life have reason to be afraid of death, because they're in fear of their sins. But first of all you're an unbeliever, and second of all—what sort of sins do you have? You've served twenty-five years in the justice department—that's all.

SORIN

(Laughs) Twenty-eight . . .

Treplyov enters and sits on a stool at Sorin's feet. Masha never takes her eyes off him.

DORN

We're keeping Konstantin Gavrilych from his work.

TREPLYOV

No, it's nothing.

Pause.

MEDVEDENKO

If I may ask, doctor, [how much does a ream of writing paper cost abroad?

DORN

I don't know. I never bought any.

MEDVEDENKO

And] which city abroad did you like the most?

DORN

Genoa.

TREPLYOV

Why Genoa?

DORN

The crowds in the street there are superb. When you step out of your hotel in the evening, the whole street is filled with people. You move aimlessly in the crowd, meandering here and there, you live with it, your psyche merges with it, and you begin to believe that there really may be one universal soul, as Nina Zarechnaya once acted in your play. Incidentally, where is Miss Zarechnaya now? And how is she?

TREPLYOV

In good health, I suppose.

DORN

I'm told she's been leading some peculiar sort of life. What's that about?

TREPLYOV

It's a long story, doctor.

DORN

Make it shorter.

Pause.

TREPLYOV

She ran away from home and took up with Trigorin. You know that?

DORN

Yes, I do.

TREPLYOV

She had a baby. The baby died. Trigorin fell out of love with her
and went back to his former attachments, as was to be expected.
In fact he never abandoned the former ones, but, being spineless,
somehow managed both this and that. As far as I can tell from what
I know, Nina's personal life has been totally unsuccessful.

DORN

And the stage?

TREPLYOV

Even worse, it seems. She made her debut at a summer theater in
a Moscow suburb, then left for the provinces. I never let her out of
my sight then; for a while I went wherever she did. She kept taking
on major roles, but she acted crudely, tastelessly, with howls and
abrupt gestures. There were moments when she exclaimed with
talent, died with talent, but they were only moments.

DORN

So anyhow there's talent?

TREPLYOV

It was hard to tell. I suppose there is. I saw her, but she didn't
want to see me, and the hotel maid wouldn't let me go to her room.
I understood how she felt and didn't insist on meeting her.

Pause.

What else can I tell you? Later, when I had already come back
home, I received letters from her. They were intelligent, warm,

interesting; she didn't complain, but I felt she was deeply unhappy, that every line spoke of sick, strained nerves. And her imagination was slightly disordered. She signed herself "Seagull." The miller in *The Water Nymph*[19] says he's a raven, and she kept repeating in her letters that she was a seagull. She's here now.

DORN

What do you mean, here?

TREPLYOV

In town, at the inn. For five days now she's been living in a room there. I went to see her, and Marya Ilyinichna here also went, but she doesn't receive anybody. Semyon Semyonych insists that yesterday after dinner he saw her in a field a mile from here.

MEDVEDENKO

Yes, I saw her. She was going the other way, towards town. I greeted her and asked why she doesn't come to visit us. She said she would.

TREPLYOV

She won't.

Pause.

Her father and stepmother don't want to know anything about her. They've set watchmen everywhere, to keep her from coming anywhere near the house. *(Goes over to the desk with the doctor)* How easy it is, doctor, to be a philosopher on paper, and how hard it is in reality!

SORIN

She was a lovely girl.

DORN

What's that, sir?

SORIN

I said, she was a lovely girl. The actual state councillor Sorin was even in love with her for a time.

DORN

Old philanderer.

Shamraev's laughter is heard.

POLINA ANDREEVNA

It seems they've come from the station . . .

TREPLYOV

Yes, I can hear mama.

Enter Arkadina and Trigorin, followed by Shamraev.

SHAMRAEV

(Entering) We keep getting older, worn down by the elements, but you, my most esteemed lady, are still young . . . Bright-colored blouse, lively . . . graceful . . .

ARKADINA

Again you're going to bring me bad luck, you tiresome man.

TRIGORIN

(To Sorin) Greetings, Pyotr Nikolaich! What's this with you feeling sick all the time? It's not good! *(Seeing Masha, joyfully)* Marya Ilyinichna!

MASHA

You recognized me? *(Shakes hands with him)*

TRIGORIN

Married?

MASHA

Long ago.

TRIGORIN

Happy? *(Greets Dorn and Medvedenko, then hesitantly goes up to Treplyov)* Irina Nikolaevna said you've forgotten the past and stopped being angry.

Treplyov holds out his hand to him.

ARKADINA

(To her son) Boris Alexeich has brought the journal with your new story in it.

TREPLYOV

(Accepting the book, to Trigorin) I thank you. You're very kind.

They sit down.

TRIGORIN

Your admirers send their greetings . . . In Petersburg and Moscow everybody's interested in you, and they keep asking me about you. They ask: what's he like, how old is he, is he dark-haired or blond? They all think for some reason that you're not young. And nobody knows your real last name, since you publish under a pen name. You're as mysterious as the Man in the Iron Mask.

TREPLYOV

Will you be with us long?

TRIGORIN

No, tomorrow I think I'll go to Moscow. I must. I'm hurrying to finish a novella, and I've also promised to contribute something to a collection. In short—the same old thing.

*While they talk, Arkadina and Polina Andreevna set up a card table
in the middle of the room; Shamraev lights candles, places chairs;
they bring a game of lotto from the cupboard.*

The weather's given me an unfriendly welcome. Biting wind.
Tomorrow morning, if it quiets down, I'll go to the lake and fish. By
the way, I must have a look at the garden and that place—remember?—where your play was performed. The motif is ripe, all I need
is to refresh the setting in my memory.

MASHA

(To her father) Papa, let my husband have a horse! He's got to go
home.

SHAMRAEV

(Imitating her) A horse . . . home . . . *(Sternly)* You saw yourself: we
just sent horses to the station. We can't drive them again.

MASHA

But there are other horses . . . *(Seeing that her father is silent, she
waves her hand)* Who can deal with you . . .

[SHAMRAEV

(Flaring up, in a low voice) So tear me to pieces! Hang me! Let
him walk!]

MEDVEDENKO

I'll walk, Masha. Really . . .

POLINA ANDREEVNA

(Sighing) Walk, in such weather . . . *(Sits down at the card table)*
Let's begin, ladies and gentlemen.

MEDVEDENKO

It's only four miles . . . Good-bye . . . *(Kisses his wife's hand)* Good-bye, mother.

His mother-in-law reluctantly offers him her hand for a kiss.

I wouldn't want to trouble anybody—it's the baby . . . *(Makes his bows to everyone)* Good-bye . . . *(Exits at a guilty pace)*

SHAMRAEV

He'll make it all right. He's not a general.

[DORN

A wife's a new life. What's become of those atoms, substances, Flammarion[20] . . .]

POLINA ANDREEVNA

(Tapping on the table) Let's begin, ladies and gentlemen. Don't waste time, dinner will be served soon.

Shamraev, Masha and Dorn sit down at the table.

ARKADINA

(To Trigorin) When the long autumn evenings come, they play lotto here. Look at this: it's the old lotto my late mother used to play with us when we were children. Would you like to play a game with us before dinner? *(She and Trigorin sit down at the table)* It's a boring game, but it's all right once you get used to it. *(Deals three lotto cards to each of them)*

TREPLYOV

(Leafing through the journal) He read his own story and didn't even cut the pages of mine. *(Puts the journal on the desk, then goes to the door left; passing his mother, he kisses her on the head)*

ARKADINA

And you, Kostya?

TREPLYOV

Sorry, I don't feel like it . . . I'll take a walk. *(Exits)*

ARKADINA

The ante is ten kopecks. Ante up for me, doctor.

DORN

Yes, ma'am.

MASHA

Has everybody anted up? I'll begin . . . Twenty-two!

ARKADINA

Got it.

MASHA

Three! . . .

DORN

Right, miss.

MASHA

You put down three? Eight! Eighty-one! Ten!

SHAMRAEV

Not so fast.

ARKADINA

How they received me in Kharkov, goodness, my head's still spinning!

MASHA

Thirty-four!

A melancholy waltz plays offstage.

ARKADINA

The students gave me an ovation . . . Three baskets of flowers, two wreaths, and this . . . *(Takes a brooch from her breast and tosses it on the table)*

SHAMRAEV

Yes, that's quite something . . .

MASHA

Fifty! . . .

DORN

Fifty exactly?

ARKADINA

I was wearing an astonishing outfit . . . Say what you like, I'm no fool when it comes to clothes.

POLINA ANDREEVNA

Kostya's playing. The poor boy's feeling sad.

SHAMRAEV

The newspapers criticize him a lot.

MASHA

Seventy-seven!

ARKADINA

Who pays attention to critics!

TRIGORIN

He has no luck. He can't find his own real voice. There's something strange, indefinite, sometimes even like delirium. Not a single living character.

MASHA

Eleven!

ARKADINA

(Looking around at Sorin) Petrusha, are you bored?

Pause.

He's asleep.

DORN

The actual state councillor is asleep.

MASHA

Seven! Ninety!

TRIGORIN

If I lived on an estate like this, by a lake, would I be writing? I'd overcome this passion in myself and do nothing but fish.

MASHA

Twenty-eight!

TRIGORIN

To catch a ruffe or a perch is such bliss!

DORN

Well, I believe in Konstantin Gavrilych. There's something there! Something there! He thinks in images, his stories are colorful, vivid, and I feel them strongly. It's just a pity he doesn't have a definite purpose. He makes an impression but nothing more, and you can't get far on impressions alone. Irina Nikolaevna, are you glad your son is a writer?

ARKADINA

Just imagine, I haven't read him yet. There's never any time.

MASHA

Twenty-six!

Treplyov enters quietly and goes to his desk.

SHAMRAEV

(To Trigorin) And we've got something of yours, Boris Alexeich.

TRIGORIN

Which thing?

SHAMRAEV

Konstantin Gavrilych once shot a seagull, and you told me to have it stuffed.

TRIGORIN

I don't remember. *(Reflecting)* I don't remember!

MASHA

Sixty-six! One!

TREPLYOV

(Throws the window open, listens) How dark! I don't understand why I feel so restless.

ARKADINA

Kostya, close the window, it's blowing.

Treplyov closes the window.

MASHA

Eighty-eight!

TRIGORIN

I win, ladies and gentlemen.

ARKADINA

(Happily) Bravo! Bravo!

SHAMRAEV

Bravo!

ARKADINA

This man is lucky always and everywhere. *(Gets up)* And now let's go and have a bite to eat. Our celebrity hasn't eaten today. We'll play more after dinner. *(To her son)* Kostya, leave your manuscripts, let's go and eat.

TREPLYOV

I don't want to, mama, I'm not hungry.

ARKADINA

As you like. [*(Wakes up Sorin)* Petrusha, dinnertime!] *(Takes Shamraev under the arm)* I'll tell you how they received me in Kharkov . . .

Polina Andreevna puts out the candles on the table, then she and Dorn push the wheelchair. They all exit left; Treplyov remains onstage alone at his desk.

[Polina puts out the candles on the table. They all exit left. Onstage remain only Sorin in his wheelchair and Treplyov at his desk.]

TREPLYOV

(Prepares to write; looks through what is already written) I've talked so much about new forms, and now I feel I'm gradually sliding into the rut myself. *(Reads)* "The poster on the fence announced . . . A pale face framed by dark hair . . ." Announced, framed . . . It's giftless. *(Crosses it out)* I'll begin with the hero being awakened by the sound of rain, and cut all the rest. The description of the moonlit evening is too long and elaborate. Trigorin has worked out his technique, so it's easy for him . . . He has the neck of a broken bottle glistening on a dam, and the black shadow of a mill wheel—there's your readymade moonlit night, while I have tremulous light, the gentle glimmer of stars, and the distant sounds of a grand piano dying away in the quiet, fragrant air . . . It's excruciating.

Pause.

Yes, I'm coming more and more to the conviction that it's not all about old and new forms, but about a man writing without thinking of any forms, writing because it pours freely from his soul.

Someone knocks on the window closest to the desk.

What's that? *(Looks out the window)* Can't see anything . . . *(Opens the glass door and looks into the garden)* Somebody ran down the steps. *(Calls out)* Who's there? *(Goes out; his quick steps are heard on the terrace; half a minute later he comes back with Nina)* Nina! Nina!

Nina leans her head on his chest and sobs with restraint.

(Moved) Nina! Nina! It's you . . . you . . . I just knew it, all day my soul has been terribly tormented. *(He takes off her hat and cape)* Oh, my good one, my beauty, she's come! We won't cry, we won't.

NINA

Somebody's here.

TREPLYOV

No, nobody. [It's my uncle. He's asleep.]

NINA

Lock the door, so they won't come in.

TREPLYOV

Nobody will come in.

NINA

I know Irina Nikolaevna's here. Lock the door . . .

TREPLYOV

(Locks the door right with a key, goes to the door left) There's no lock on this one. I'll put a chair up against it. *(Puts the armchair against the door)* Don't be afraid, nobody will come in.

NINA

(Looks intently in his face) Let me look at you. [And now at him. *(Goes to Sorin)* Asleep.] *(Glances around)* Warm, nice . . . This used to be the drawing room. Have I changed a lot?

TREPLYOV

Yes . . . You've grown thinner, and your eyes got bigger. Nina, it's somehow strange to be looking at you. Why wouldn't you let me see you? Why didn't you come before now? I know you've been living here for almost a week . . . I went to you several times each day, stood under your window like a beggar.

NINA

I was afraid you hated me. Every night I dream that you look at me and don't recognize me. If you only knew! I've been walking around here ever since I came . . . by the lake. I've passed by your house many times but couldn't bring myself to come in. Let's sit down.

They sit down.

We'll sit and talk and talk. It's so nice here, warm, cozy . . . Do you hear the wind? Turgenev says somewhere: "Lucky the one who on such a night has a roof over his head, a warm corner to sit in."[21] I'm the seagull . . . No, it's not that. *(Rubs her forehead)* What was I talking about? Ah, yes . . . Turgenev . . . "And may the Lord help all homeless wanderers . . ." Never mind. *(Sobs)*

TREPLYOV

Nina, again you . . . Nina!

NINA

Never mind, it makes me feel better . . . I haven't cried for two years. Late yesterday evening I went to the garden, to see if our theater was there. And it's still standing. I cried for the first time in two years, and I was relieved, it all became clearer to me. You see, I'm not crying anymore. *(Takes his hand)* So you've become a writer . . . You're a writer, I'm an actress . . . We're both caught in the whirl . . . I used to live joyfully, like a child—woke up in the morning and sang; loved you, dreamed of fame, and now? Early tomorrow morning I've got to go to Eletz, third class . . . with the peasants, and in Eletz the educated merchants will pester me with their courtesies. Life is rough!

TREPLYOV

Why to Eletz?

NINA

I've taken an engagement for the whole winter. It's time for me to go. [*(Nods toward Sorin)* Is it bad?

TREPLYOV

Yes. *(Pause)*] Nina, I cursed you, hated you, tore up your letters and photographs, but I was aware every moment that my soul is bound to you forever. I can't stop loving you, Nina. Ever since I lost you and began to publish, life has been unbearable for me— I suffer . . . It's as if my youth was suddenly torn away, and it seems to me that I've already lived in this world for ninety years. I call out to you, I kiss the ground you've walked on; wherever I look, I see your face, that gentle smile, which shone upon me in the best years of my life . . .

NINA

(At a loss) Why does he talk like this, why does he talk like this?

TREPLYOV

I'm alone, I'm not warmed by anyone's affection, I'm as cold as if I'm buried, and whatever I write, it's all dry, stale, dark. Stay here, Nina, I beg you, or else let me go with you!

Nina quickly puts on her hat and cape.

Why, Nina? For God's sake, Nina . . . *(Watches her dress; pause)*

NINA

My horses are at the gate. Don't see me off, I'll go by myself . . .
(Through tears) Give me some water . . .

TREPLYOV

(Gives her water) Where are you going now?

NINA

To town.

Pause.

So Irina Nikolaevna's here?

TREPLYOV

Yes . . . my uncle fell ill on Thursday, we sent a telegram telling her
to come.

NINA

Why do you say you kissed the ground I walked on? I ought to
be killed. *(Leans over the desk)* I'm so tired! If only I could rest . . .
rest! *(Raises her head)* I'm the seagull . . . It's not that. I'm an
actress. Right! *(Hearing Arkadina's and Trigorin's laughter, listens, then runs to door left and looks through the keyhole)* He's here,
too . . . *(Goes back to Treplyov)* Right . . . Never mind . . . Right . . .
He didn't believe in the theater, kept laughing at my dreams, and
little by little I also stopped believing and lost heart . . . And then
there were the cares of love, jealousy, constant fear for the little one
. . . I became trivial, worthless, I performed mindlessly . . . I didn't
know what to do with my hands, didn't know how to stand on
the stage, couldn't control my voice. You don't understand what
it's like when you feel that your acting is terrible. I'm the seagull.
No, it's not that. Remember you shot a seagull? A man happened
along, saw it, and, having nothing better to do, destroyed . . . A
subject for a short story. It's not that . . . *(Rubs her forehead)* What
was I talking about? . . . About the stage. I'm not like that now . . .

I'm a real actress, I act with delight, in rapture, I get intoxicated onstage and feel that I'm beautiful. And now, being here, I keep walking, walking and thinking, thinking and feeling how my inner strength keeps growing every day . . . Now I know, I understand, Kostya, that in our kind of work—whether it's acting onstage or writing—the main thing is not fame, not glitter, not what I used to dream about, but being able to endure. Being able to bear your cross and believe. I believe, and now it's not so painful for me, and when I remember my calling, I'm not afraid of life.

TREPLYOV

(Sadly) You've found your way, you know where you're going, and I'm still drifting in a chaos of fantasies and images, not knowing why or who needs it. I don't believe, and I don't know what my calling is.

NINA

(Listening) Shh . . . I'm going. Good-bye. When I become a great actress, come and take a look at me. Promise? And now . . . *(Presses his hand)* It's already late. I can barely stand up . . . I'm exhausted, I want to eat . . .

TREPLYOV

Stay, I'll give you supper . . .

NINA

No, no . . . Don't see me off, I'll go by myself . . . My horses are just nearby . . . So she brought him with her? Well, it makes no difference. When you see Trigorin, don't tell him anything . . . I love him. I love him even more than before . . . A subject for a short story . . . I love him, love him passionately, love him to despair. How good things used to be, Kostya! Remember? What a clear, warm, joyful, pure life, and what feelings—feelings like tender, graceful flowers . . . Remember? . . . *(Recites)* [*(Sits down on a little stool, takes a sheet from the bed and throws it over herself)*] "People, lions, eagles and partridges, antlered deer, geese, spiders, silent fish inhabiting the waters, starfish and those not visible to the eye—in short, all living things, all living things, all living things have completed their sad round and are extinct . . . For thousands of years already the earth has not borne upon itself a single living being, and this poor moon lights its lamp in vain. The cranes no longer awaken with a cry in the meadows, nor are the june bugs heard in the linden groves . . ." *(Embraces Treplyov impulsively and runs out through the glass door)* [*(Throws off the sheet, impulsively embraces Treplyov, and runs out through the glass door)*]

TREPLYOV

(After a pause) It will be bad if somebody meets her in the garden and then tells mama. It might upset her . . .

For the next two minutes he silently tears up all his manuscripts and throws them under the desk, then unlocks the door right and exits.

DORN

(Trying to open the door left) Strange. The door seems to be locked . . . *(Enters and puts the armchair back in place)* An obstacle course.

[POLINA ANDREEVNA

(Enters after him) You looked at her all the time. I beg you, I beseech you by all that's holy, don't torment me. Don't look at her, don't talk to her for so long.

DORN

All right, I'll try.

POLINA ANDREEVNA

(Pressing his hand to her breast) I know my jealousy is stupid, senseless. I myself am ashamed. You're sick of me.

DORN

No, never mind. If it's hard for you to be quiet, go on talking.]

Enter Arkadina,[Polina Andreevna,] followed by Yakov, with bottles, and Masha, then Shamraev and Trigorin.

ARKADINA

Put the red wine and the beer for Boris Alexeich here on the table. We'll play and drink. Let's sit down, ladies and gentlemen.

POLINA ANDREEVNA

(To Yakov) Serve the tea now, too. *(Lights the candles, sits down at the card table)*

SHAMRAEV

(Leads Trigorin over to the cupboard) Here's the thing I was talking about earlier ... *(Takes the stuffed seagull out of the cupboard)* You ordered it.

TRIGORIN

(Looking at the seagull) I don't remember! *(Reflects)* I don't remember!

A gunshot offstage right. Everybody jumps.

ARKADINA

(Frightened) What was that?

DORN

Nothing. Something must have exploded in my medicine bag. Don't worry. *(Exits through door right, comes back half a minute later)* That was it. A vial of ether exploded. *(Softly sings)* "Again I stand before thee enchanted ..."

ARKADINA

(Sitting down at the table) Phew, I got scared. It reminded me of ... *(Covers her face with her hands)* Everything even went dark ...

DORN

(Leafing through the journal, to Trigorin) A couple of months ago they published an article . . . a letter from America, and by the way I wanted to ask you . . . *(Puts his arm around Trigorin's waist and leads him downstage)* Because this question interests me very much . . . *(Lowers his voice, in a half whisper)* Take Irina Nikola-evna away somewhere . . . The thing is, Konstantin Gavrilych just shot himself . . .

CURTAIN

NOTES

1. It's in mourning for my life: Masha, or Chekhov, borrows these
   words from the novel *Bel Ami* (1885), by Guy de Maupassant
   (1850–1893), in which, toward the end of chapter 7, a woman
   explains why she wears black: *Je suis arrivée à l'âge où on fait
   le deuil de sa vie.* ("I've reached the age at which one mourns
   for one's life.")
2. Nekrasov . . . Duse . . . *La dame aux camélias* . . . *The Fumes
   of Life*: Nikolai Nekrasov (1821–1878), poet, critic, radical
   thinker and editor, was the author of a number of long poems
   on social themes. Eleonora Duse (1858–1924), Italian actress,
   became one of the most prominent figures in the theater of her
   time, a rival of the famous French actress Sarah Bernhardt.
   Chekhov saw and admired her when she toured Russia in
   1891. *La dame aux camélias*, a novel by Alexandre Dumas,
   fils (1824–1895), published in 1848 and adapted for the stage
   by the author in 1852, remained his most popular work. Sarah
   Bernhardt and Eleonora Duse both acted in the play, and it
   served as the basis for Verdi's opera *La Traviata*. *The Fumes of*

Life, by the conservative Russian novelist Boleslaw Markevich (1822–1884), was adapted for the stage by the author from his novel *The Abyss*. Chekhov detested the play (as well as the novel) and thought of writing a parody of it.

3. Maupassant . . . the Eiffel Tower: Maupassant was a member of a committee (Dumas, *fils* was another) that petitioned against the building of the Eiffel Tower. He used to eat in a restaurant at the foot of the tower, the one place in Paris from which it was impossible to see it.

4. "To France two grenadiers . . .": "The Two Grenadiers" (*"Die beiden Grenadiere"*) is a romance by Heinrich Heine (1797–1856), set to music by Robert Schumann (1810–1856).

5. "Say not your youth was ruined . . .": Words from the poem "A Sick Man's Jealousy," by Nikolai Nekrasov (see note 2), set to music by Yakov Prigozhy (1840–1920).

6. "Again I stand before thee . . .": Opening words of the poem "Stanzas" (1842), by Vasilii Ivanovich Krasov (1820–1855), set to music by Alexander Alyabyev (1787–1851). The full line is, "Again I stand before you enchanted . . ."

7. Chadin . . . Raspluev . . . Sadovsky: Prov Sadovsky (1818–1872) was a prominent actor in the famous Maly Theatre in Moscow. Raspluev is a character in the play *Krechinsky's Wedding*, by Alexander Sukhovo-Kobylin (1817–1903). Chadin seems to be Chekhov's invention.

8. *De gustibus . . . nihil*: Shamraev fuses and slightly distorts two Latin sayings: *De gustibus non est disputandum* ("There is no disputing about taste") and *De mortuis aut bene aut nihil* ("Of the dead [speak] either good or nothing").

9. My son! . . . nasty sty: *Hamlet*, Act III, scene iv, lines 89–95 (slightly modified), spoken by Hamlet's mother Gertrude and by Hamlet himself.

10. Thou art angry, Jupiter . . . : The full saying is "Thou art angry, Jupiter, therefore thou art wrong." The ultimate source of the saying is unknown, but it became popular in Russia. Dostoevsky gives it to the lawyer Fetyukovich toward the end of *The Brothers Karamazov*.

11. The *jeune premier*: The young male lead or young lover in French plays.

12. "Tell it to her, my flowers . . .": From the aria *Faites-lui mes aveux*, sung by the young Siébel to the bouquet he leaves for Marguerite in Act III of the opera *Faust* (1859), by Charles Gounod (1818–1893).

13. The passage comes from Maupassant's *Sur l'eau (On the Water*, 1888), a prose piece describing a cruise along the Côte d'Azur, mixed with various reflections.

14. Buckle and Spencer: Henry Thomas Buckle (1821–1862), British historian, often called "the father of scientific history," was the author of *History of Civilization in England* (volume I published in 1857, volume II in 1861; left unfinished at his death) in which he sought the "fixed and regular" laws that govern human action. Herbert Spencer (1820–1903), British philosopher and political theorist, was a utilitarian and social evolutionist; it was he, not Darwin, who coined the phrase "survival of the fittest."

15. Poprishchin: Aksenty Ivanovich Poprishchin is the narrator/ protagonist of "The Diary of a Madman" (1835) by Nikolai Gogol (1809–1852).

16. on four . . . evening: The riddle ("What goes on four legs in the morning, two legs at noon, and three legs in the evening?") is posed to Oedipus by the Sphinx in Sophocles's *Oedipus the King*. (The answer is "Man.")

17. *The Great Mail Robbery*: A notorious robbery and mistrial in France, in 1796, made into a melodrama in 1850 with the title *L'affaire du courrier de Lyon (The Affair of the Lyons Mail*), adapted into Russian as *The Great Mail Robbery*. Chekhov saw it as a teenager.

18. "The moon . . . sky . . .": The opening line of the serenade *Tigrenok (The Tiger Cub*), by Konstantin Stepanovich Shilovsky (1849–1893), a minor composer and librettist best known for his work with Tchaikovsky.

19. *The Water Nymph*: A verse drama by Alexander Pushkin (1799–1837), based on folktale motifs: when a miller's daughter is betrayed by her princely lover and drowns herself, her

father goes mad, believes he is a raven, and presents himself to
the guilty prince, shrieking and denouncing him.

20. Flammarion: Camille Flammarion (1842–1925) was a French
astronomer and science fiction writer, who sought to combine
scientific method with the popular spiritism of his time.

21. Turgenev says somewhere: The quotations, slightly altered,
come from the epilogue to *Rudin* (1856), the first novel of Ivan
Sergeevich Turgenev (1818–1883).

ANTON PAVLOVICH CHEKHOV (1860–1904) was born in Taganrog, on the Sea of Azov. His grandfather was a serf, but managed to buy his freedom and that of his family some years before the abolition of serfdom by the emperor Alexander II in 1861. Chekhov attended the Greek high school in Taganrog, and, on graduating in 1879, went on to study medicine in Moscow. In that same year he wrote his first play, entitled *Fatherlessness* and later known as *Platonov*, after the central character. It was never published or performed in his lifetime, but has recently been produced to great acclaim. To support himself in medical school, Chekhov wrote comic sketches for the newspapers, as he had done earlier in Taganrog, but by the time he graduated in 1884, writing had become a more serious matter for him. In that same year he first showed symptoms of the tuberculosis that was to cut short his life. In 1887 a theater director in Moscow commissioned a play from him, and ten days later Chekhov gave him *Ivanov*, which was produced with success in Moscow and a year later in Petersburg. He also wrote a number of one-act comic sketches during those years. Then in 1894 he wrote *The Seagull*, the first of the four great plays that have since become central works of modern theater. The original production, in Petersburg, was disappointing, especially for Chekhov, but the play was noticed by Vladimir Nemirovich-Danchenko, co-founder with Konstantin Stanislavsky of the new Moscow Art Theatre. Their production in 1898 was a triumph and is now recognized as one of the greatest events in Russian, and world, theater. Chekhov's next play, *Uncle Vanya*, was published in 1897 and produced by the Moscow Art Theatre in 1899. It was followed by *Three Sisters* in 1901 and, finally, by *The Cherry Orchard* in 1904. During the spring of that year, Chekhov's tuberculosis became critical; he went to a sanatorium in Badenweiler, in the Black Forest, and died there in mid-July.

RICHARD NELSON's plays include the four-play series *The Apple Family: Scenes from Life in the Country* (*That Hopey Changey Thing*, *Sweet and Sad*, *Sorry* and *Regular Singing*), *Nikolai and the Others*, *Farewell to the Theatre, Conversations in Tusculum, How Shakespeare Won the West, Frank's Home, Rodney's Wife, Franny's Way, Madame Melville, Goodnight Children Everywhere, New England, The General from America, Misha's Party* (with Alexander Gelman), *Two Shakespearean Actors* and *Some Americans Abroad.* He has written the musicals *James Joyce's The Dead* (with Shaun Davey) and *My Life with Albertine* (with Ricky Ian Gordon), and the screenplays for the films *Hyde Park-on-Hudson* and *Ethan Frome.* He has received numerous awards, including a Tony (Best Book of a Musical for *James Joyce's The Dead*), an Olivier (Best Play for *Goodnight Children Everywhere*) and two New York Drama Critics' Circle Awards (*James Joyce's The Dead* and *The Apple Family*). He is the recipient of the PEN/ Laura Pels Master Playwright Award, an Academy Award from the American Academy of Arts and Letters; he is an Honorary Associate Artist of the Royal Shakespeare Company. He lives in upstate New York.

RICHARD PEVEAR was born in Boston, grew up on Long Island, attended Allegheny College (BA 1964) and the University of Virginia (MA 1965). After a stint as a college teacher, he moved to the Maine coast and eventually to New York City, where he worked as a freelance writer, editor and translator, and also as a cabinetmaker. He has published two collections of poetry, many essays and reviews, and some thirty books translated from French, Italian and Russian.

LARISSA VOLOKHONSKY was born in Leningrad, attended Leningrad State University and, on graduating, joined a scientific team whose work took her to the far east of Russia, to Kamchatka and Sakhalin Island. She emigrated to Israel in 1973, and to the United States in 1975, where she attended Yale Divinity School and St. Vladimir's Theological Seminary. Soon after settling in New York City, she married Richard Pevear, and a few years later they moved to France with their two children.

Together, Pevear and Volokhonsky have translated twenty books from the Russian, including works by Fyodor Dostoevsky, Leo Tolstoy, Mikhail Bulgakov, Anton Chekhov, Boris Pasternak and Nikolai Leskov. Their translation of Dostoevsky's *The Brothers Karamazov* received the PEN Translation Prize for 1991; their translation of Tolstoy's *Anna Karenina* was awarded the same prize in 2002; and in 2006 they were awarded the first Efim Etkind International Translation Prize by the European University of St. Petersburg.